SALARIUS

AN INAMORATA NOVELLA

SALARIUS

AN INAMORATA NOVELLA

NAKIA COOK

VEILED THREATS PUBLICATIONS

Salarius: An Inamorata Novella

First edition April 2023

Veiled Threats Publications

ISBN 978-1-7774039-6-6 (e-book)

ISBN 978-1-7774039-7-3 (paperback)

ISBN 978-1-7774039-8-0 (hardcover)

ALSO BY NAKIA COOK

Inamorata: A Rosewood Hollow Novel

Drummer Boy: A Short Story

For my Family and the readers who've touched my heart. Thank you for your support.

salarius: adjective. fr. salarius belonging to salt, fr. sal salt.

"You can prevent meat from rotting with salt, but what can prevent salt from rotting?

Afghan Proverb.

Prologue

It would serve him right if the smoldering dark oak beams on the ceiling fell and crushed the life out of him. He ran towards the front door and could feel the demonic man gaining on him.

He prayed the fire would grow. With a little luck, his problems would go up in smoke. Shame washed over him as flames licked the roof. *She's young. She'll bounce back from this.* No matter how he told the lie, he couldn't quite convince himself.

He made it outside. And so did the demon. Glass flew everywhere around them, slicing his cheekbones and the exposed flesh of his hands as he shielded his eyes. He recalled the way his cousin had fretted over this restaurant for six months before it opened. Mumtaz had destroyed it in a week. Poor girl. He didn't want to be around when she learned about the blaze.

Sirens wailed in the distance. He hoped they were far enough away that the restaurant burned to the ground first. The flames reflected off the brickwork of nearby buildings. Time was running out. Panic rose in his chest.

For a moment, the tightness in his palms stole his attention. Time stopped, and he stared at the lack of creases in his hands, marveling at how smooth they looked without their lifelines.

His mother had once told him that greed turns people into monsters; that once they'd had a taste, there was no turning back. He'd taken her words with a grain of salt. Now, he knew better.

Chapter One

"Do you mind? I'm in the middle of something." Monet Tansy shoved a wandering hand away from her breast and continued gathering dirt and dust off the surface of the gravestone in front of her.

"I'm trying to be in the middle of something too," Mumtaz Busri said, nibbling at her earlobe. She swatted at him, and when it did no good, launched an elbow at a tender spot in his ribcage.

"Ow! Don't be like that, Mo," Mumtaz said, rubbing his chest as he backed away from her. "I need something to take my mind off my troubles."

"What troubles?" she asked, studying the grave.

"Weren't you listening before?"

"Not really." She loosened the dirt at her feet with the toe of one of her red boots.

Mumtaz sighed. "Damn, woman, I told you I needed you to check out my hands." He showed her his palms, but she busied herself with an interesting spot on the ground. "Hello? Earth to Monet. Come in, please."

"I'm busy, Taz. Give me a minute." Monet crouched to swipe a handful of dust and earth from the foot of the gravestone, and dropped it into a green silken drawstring pouch, then pulled the strings taut and tied them into a bow. She tucked the small package into the pocket of her red duster and clapped her hands together three times over the base of the headstone before rising.

"Not this Voodoo shit again," Mumtaz said, rolling his eyes.

"Hoodoo," she corrected.

"Whatever. I don't believe in either. What's the difference anyway?" he asked.

Monet met his dark brown eyes with her own and smirked. "Chile, if only you knew," she said, in a lilted accent. "I find it ironic that you want me to use my gift on your hands while you turn your nose up at it. And since when do you believe in anything?"

"Hey, I might not be the most practicing Muslim, but I know not to mess around with whatever it is you're doing to that grave. And I'm not asking you to use your so-called gift for diagnosing my hands. I just want you to look at it. You're a nurse, can't you help a brother out?"

"Liar. We both know you've been to every doctor who would listen. You want some of my juju."

"Whatever," he said, not meeting her eyes.

He watched her reach into another hidden pocket in her long, thin coat and grimaced. He hated that coat, and she wore it everywhere, even in hot weather. Simple acts, like pulling out impossibly large objects from its invisible compartments, made him question his grip on reality.

Even the texture of it freaked him out. It felt like skin. Not like a cow's leather, or the buttery feel of lambskin, but actual skin. *Human skin.* Mumtaz shuddered.

This time, she produced a gnarly-stemmed flower, its petals in perfect condition. Mumtaz forgot himself, dropping his hands to his sides as he studied it over her shoulder. He'd never seen anything like the thorny black monstrosity. The petals, black as the fabric of the night sky, were substantial, thick, and veiny. Like the flesh of her jacket.

He watched her tear the leaves apart and sprinkle them over the grassy mound between her red heels. When she finished, her fingertips were red and moist. Bloody-looking, like her boots.

Mumtaz squinted against the sunshine and read the name etched into the gravestone. "Hey, who is Marissa Shelby? Did you have some beef with her?"

"What I'm doing is not harming Marissa Shelby," Monet said, approaching him with her hands in her pockets. Mumtaz backed away, uncertain. He'd known Monet long enough to share her bed, but not long enough to trust her.

"But somebody is being harmed, right?" He inhaled and exhaled slowly as she withdrew her empty hands from her pockets and reached for one of his. They were clean again, showing no trace of the red stains. Magical pockets.

"Why do you care?" she asked, tracing her index finger over the palm of his left hand in intricate patterns. He wiggled his fingers in response. "Hold still, Taz."

"I'm trying, but you're tickling me. How does it look?"

"Damn, I'm checking," she said, studying the lines on the inside of his hand.

"Are you getting the precise measurements or something?"

"Shh. Taz, just wait."

Mumtaz rolled his eyes. He let her explore both sides of his hand and found himself disgusted and delighted by her touch. A year ago, had someone told him he'd be having a fling with a beautiful, brown-skinned witchy nurse, he would have pissed himself laughing. But here he was, half-afraid of her, mostly aroused, and completely captivated.

The doctors told him that hands change over time, sometimes developing new lines in the palm. It was rare, but no big deal. None of them could answer why the lifeline was fading altogether, the pigment and the creases too. He would never have noticed if it hadn't felt tight when he extended his hands, like he'd spread super glue over the palms and allowed them to dry.

His mother, ever vehement, prompted him to get another opinion. He relented, but only after medicine failed him. "Seek help at this address, Mumtaz," the imam at her favorite mosque had said as he scribbled an address on the back of a business card. Mumtaz went there seeking an exorcism. Instead, eviction notices on the door led him back to the elevator, exasperated. The doors opened, and Monet stood there looking like she had been waiting for him all his life. *Destiny lies at the feet of this woman,* he told himself.

"It's still getting shorter, Taz."

"Shit," he said, jerking his hand away. "Are you sure? Maybe we should take pictures to compare it next time. You know, see if we can tell that it shrinks."

"We don't need pictures, Taz. The line is shorter. The last time, it was just under your pinky. Now it's between your ring finger and your pinky." Monet swept her thick black braids into a ponytail. He hoped she would take them down soon. Her lush, spiral curls drove him wild. "Your lifeline is shrinking. Nothing I can do about that," she said, shrugging.

"Maybe I should get a second opinion. You got any friends who read palms?" Mumtaz frowned. "What's so funny?"

"I knew it, Mumtaz. You wanna dabble in the spirit world. Don't worry, I won't tell your mama."

"Girl, please. Is that supposed to scare me? I'm a grown-ass man, and my mama can mind her business."

"Uh huh. I bet you don't tell her that to her face since you're living in her home," Monet said, folding her arms across her chest.

"Okay, whatever, damn," he said, forcing a laugh. "I'll wait for you in the car."

"See you in a minute, grown-ass man," she said.

Mumtaz walked away from her in a huff toward the parking lot. He hated discussing his living situation. Making him feel small was Monet's biggest flaw. Mumtaz climbed into his ancient Toyota Celica and slammed the door. Shrinking lifeline. What did that mean?

The doctors, the imam, and now, Monet. They were all full of shit. Minus the mystery behind his smooth palms, he was in perfect health. What good was a Voodoo priestess who couldn't heal him with magic? "Hoodoo, not Voodoo," he mimicked.

He dug into his front pocket and pulled out the five-year-old cellphone he'd acquired at a swap meet. His fingers tapped at the screen until they opened the bookmarked page for his favorite off-track betting site. Sweat burst from his pores as he scrolled through the race results, searching for confirmation of his win. He'd gained inside information from a friend of a friend of the dietitian of the jockey for his favorite horse. There was no way he would lose.

"Come on, Blue Mountain, shit, shit, shit!" He tossed the phone to the floor. Sweat poured down his forehead, and he jabbed the key into the ignition and started the car. The engine wheezed in protest as he turned it a second too long. "Shut up, you old heap."

He banged on the dash harder than necessary, forcing cool air from the finicky vents. When he calmed down, his mind calculated how much he lost, and he winced. Four thousand dollars. He pictured his last bank statement and scratched at his goatee. In the rearview mirror, he glimpsed a red article of clothing. And another beside it.

Monet stood at the edge of a thicket of trees talking to a pale white woman with jet black hair in a red dress. Mumtaz adjusted the mirror to get a better look. The woman reached into Monet's green drawstring pouch and pulled out a handful of dirt. Mumtaz saw her smell it, then put it into her mouth.

A sharp crack of bones and the woman's jaw went slack. The underlying structure of bone and cartilage stretched and changed the appearance of the skin on her face. When everything settled down and found its place, her face no longer resembled itself. She had morphed into a new person.

"What the hell?" Both women shot glances toward the car. Mumtaz jerked and turned the mirror away. Had they heard him? He jumped a second time when the passenger door opened, and Monet climbed inside. "H-how did you get here so fast?" he asked, looking into the mirror once more.

"I'm sorry I took so long. We can leave now." Monet leaned across the seat and sank her fingers into the thick, spiral curls of his afro.

"Who was your friend?"

"Hmm? What friend?"

"The white woman in the red dress. I saw you talking to her."

"That was no woman," Mo said, lifting an eyebrow.

"I thought I saw her eating dirt from your bag of tricks," he said, fondling the pouch around her neck. He regretted touching the gross object and snatched his hand away. She withdrew her fingers from his hair and returned to the passenger seat.

Monet smiled. "I don't know why you're so shocked. I talk and walk with my ancestors, Taz. Sometimes they do me favors."

"Astaghfirullah," he said and wiped his hands over his face. He hoped his supplication for forgiveness reached the doorstep of the lowest heaven. He was going to need all the help he could get with Monet in his life. "Favors from the dead," he grumbled.

Monet reached down and picked up his phone from the floorboards. "Lost again, huh? Maybe you should look into more stable money-making ventures, Taz. Gambling ain't the one for you." She handed back the phone and slid a pair of red sunglasses onto her face.

"You're right. I'm thinking about getting into NFT's."

"NFT's? Do you even know what they are?"

"Yeah, some digital art shit. I might commission some starving art students to make me some pieces for twenty dollars a pop. After that, I'll throw them onto the internet. I'm bound to make a killing," he said, stroking his short stump of chin hair.

"Are you serious?"

"As a heart attack," he said.

She pulled the sunglasses down the length of her nose and considered him. "Baby, you are always a scheme away from happiness."

"Yes, I am. But what can we do about my hand, Mo? It's damned near impossible to grip the steering wheel. I mean, have you seen this before? A shrinking lifeline?"

"Once when I was a little girl."

"What happened?"

Monet flashed him a mischievous smile. When she tilted her head, the sun cast shadows across the large folds in her eyelids. Mumtaz ran a thumb along her cheek, tracing the freckles she said she'd inherited from the Creole side of her family. He didn't know which side that was since she never mentioned them again, and he'd never thought to bring it up on his own. "My daddy shot him and buried his body in the West Virginia salt caves."

He withdrew his thumb. "Damn. That's harsh. You're kidding, right?"

"Let's go, Taz. I've got one more errand before you take me to work."

Chapter Two

"OH, COME ON. SO CLOSE." Mumtaz shook his head and turned off the news radio broadcast announcing last night's Powerball numbers. He'd dropped an extra five hundred on tickets, hoping something would hit. And to boost his chances of success, he purchased three hundred dollars' worth of pull tabs from the local bingo hall. He couldn't believe that every ticket had been a bust.

"Lost again, Taz?"

He ignored her snarky grin. "What are we doing here, Mo? Are you picking up a parcel or something?" Mumtaz cut the engine as they idled in the deserted rear parking lot of White Crow Shipping and climbed out of his tired Celica. The car groaned under the shift in weight as he stepped onto the curb and slammed the door. "Piece of shit," he said to the knocking engine. "We've been driving for ten minutes. When my ship comes in, you're the first thing to go," he said, looking into the side mirror.

"You can wait here for me here, Taz. I'll only be here for a couple of minutes," Monet said, getting out of the car. She fished around in her purse, then walked toward a nondescript warehouse at the back of the lot with a yellow piece of paper in her hand.

The sun receded into the clouds, creating harsh shadows on the tilted sign hanging from the shabby-looking red and white main building. By the looks of it, he would have guessed that the place had gone out of business a long time ago. He cocked his ear at the disquieting silence, listening for birds. Despite spring's arrival, the trees, crooked, bent and barren from the harsh winter, bore no signs of life. And yet, he felt eyes on him.

"If it's all the same to you, I'll tag along," Mumtaz said. He turned up the collar of his blazer, but a sudden chill found its way into his shirt, anyway. "Do you see that?" He pointed toward an eerie, rolling mist hovering on the lawn.

"What? It's just fog." Monet kept walking.

"Look at it; it's moving like it's alive." He trotted behind her, hopping over it.

"You're so weird," Monet said, entering the warehouse.

"I'm not weird. This place is weird."

"It's cozy."

"Cozy? Aw, hell naw, Mo. I'm glad I don't have to come all the way out here to pick up my merchandise. Can you imagine how it must look at dawn? It wouldn't surprise me to see a zombie or two. What are we doing here, anyway?"

"I am minding my business, and you are tagging along uninvited, remember?" Monet rang the buzzer next to a gray door in the foyer.

"Your business is my business today, or did you forget that I drove you? And that's another thing; why don't you own a car yet?"

"I told you; I'm saving up for what I really want. There's no way I want a lemon like yours. No offense," she said.

"None taken, I know it's crap. I can't believe you've survived this long without wheels, though. It's been a year."

"I get gullible men to take care of me," she said, ringing the bell again.

"If your butt wasn't so nice, I'd leave you here for disrespecting me like that," he said, pressing his body against hers.

"No you wouldn't." She reached behind her and rubbed his cheek. "You can't stand to watch people suffer. Even when they deserve it. Hello, is anybody there?" She knocked, then stood on tiptoe and leaned against the small window next to the door, shielding the light.

"What do you see?" Mumtaz asked, blowing into his cupped hands. The temperature in the foyer felt worse than the crisp air outside. All the sweat from his gambling woes dried up on contact. His eyes dropped to the floor. "Monet, check it out. The fog is coming inside the building. Is that normal? Can fog penetrate a closed door?"

"Can I help you?" A black smiling face emerged from the mist.

"Damn, brother, you scared the hell out of me!" Mumtaz clutched his chest and backed away from the man at the door.

"May I see your waybill?" The man looked past Mumtaz and spoke to Monet. His accent sounded a bit French and something else Mumtaz couldn't place.

"It's right here," she said, approaching him with the yellow slip of paper.

Mumtaz noticed how their coats mirrored one another's, except the man's was white, as was his kinky, coiled hair and everything else, except his skin.

His bluish-black complexion reminded Mumtaz of the Senegalese merchants who sold fabric next to his mother's vegetable stall when they had lived in Mali. Thinking of them made him homesick. Not this guy though; he creeped him out. Something about his demeanor turned him off.

The man walked over to the gray door and punched in a code on the keypad. A loud hiss escaped from the warehouse as though the air had been pressurized. "Follow me," the man said, holding the door open.

"I like your coat, Lebe," Monet said as she slipped into the warehouse.

"Thank you, Monet. It's albino."

Mumtaz walked behind Monet, careful not to let Lebe's clothing touch his skin. Albino... albino what? Mumtaz felt Lebe's eyes on him as he stepped across the threshold and turned to find him watching.

He offered a slight smile, attempting to soften Lebe's hard expression, but he remained unchanged. Mumtaz's gesture fell from his lips. *Who does this guy think he is?* He shrugged it off and entered the warehouse. Lebe closed the door behind him, shutting them inside, and the air stopped circulating. Mumtaz swallowed to relieve the pressure.

His ears refused to pop, and he looked around while working his jaw, forcing himself to yawn. A loud whoosh of air opened his ears and the powerful odors of piss and animals assaulted his nostrils, and a barrage of sounds rumbled against his clogged ears. Somewhere in the dim warehouse, he could hear the call of monkeys and croaking frogs. He swore that a hyena laughed in the distance. Where were they? Some kind of zoo?

The dizzying number of ravens and parrots made up for the lack of birds outside. He saw them, not in cages, but diving and swooping from the rafters. There were other sounds that he didn't recognize; ones that made the hairs stand up on his back, but the worst, which he later convinced himself must have been his own, was the sound of a beating heart. He felt it through the warehouse floor, thumping through his shoes, which he couldn't see in the oppressive carpet of fog.

And what was with that fog, pressing against his ankles and anchoring his feet to the floor? Did fog have a weight? He didn't think so, but this one did. It felt substantial as it dashed over his shoes, like small scurrying creatures.

Mumtaz leaned against one of the never-ending rows of metal racks filled with boxes and baskets of merchandise, allowing his eyes to take it all in. There was more here than exotic animals. He thought about capturing the absurdity with his phone camera but assumed a sign warning of a firm no filming policy was in effect, like at his own warehouse.

The entire aisle held various types and sizes of sea glass, crystals, and gems in hundreds of shapes and colors. The crystals reminded him of the ones Mo ordered from a livestream on the *Vewz* social media app. The aisle extended as far as he could see, as did all the rows. He would have wagered that they stretched beyond the dimensions of the building. *It must be a trick of the light. An illusion.* Mumtaz snapped to attention as a hint of musk and sweat from Lebe's body wafted into his nostrils as the man walked to the service counter and stepped behind it.

"I have to get authorization for this order," Lebe said, scanning the paper.

"That's fine." Monet leaned on the counter.

"How long is that gonna take?" Mumtaz asked. He regretted not staying in the car but didn't want to look stupid by asking Lebe to open the door and let him out because he had a case of the willies.

"I'm not sure," Lebe said, dialing a number on his cellphone. "This is a special order for delicate contents; I need authorization to release it."

Mumtaz turned to Monet. "Baby, I can't take all day. I've got those mushrooms in the car." *And I need to get the hell out of Black Magic Costco.*

"Be cool, Taz. Let the man call it in," she purred. "You'll be fine."

"This is my livelihood we're talking about, Mo. I don't know what freaky stuff you ordered from this place, but I have business elsewhere. Proper business."

"Last night, you said you could drive me here. You said nothing about mushrooms," she said, narrowing her eyes. He could have sworn he saw purple light flash in them. "Next time, I'll call a more reliable man to help me out, okay?" She straightened up and tossed her ponytail in his direction, signaling the end of the conversation.

Lebe glanced from Monet to Mumtaz and smirked.

Mumtaz cut the tall, slender man with a look that suggested he mind his business, then he turned to Monet and considered her. What did she mean, find someone else? He usurped as much of her time as was possible to keep her away from the appreciative advances of other men. If she spent time with someone else, she was damn good at hiding it.

Still, the possibility of his replacement angered and terrified him; he wanted her all to himself. A broad smile spread across his thick brown lips, and he feigned laughter. "Stop tripping, Mo. There's nobody else more reliable than me," he said, checking his watch. He could give her another fifteen minutes.

Monet reached into a pocket and pulled out an emery board. "Nobody's tripping but you."

He sighed and shoved himself off the rack, heading toward a different row. This aisle contained items that Mumtaz would expect to find in the far corners of the internet, on sites that were hazardous for the average consumer to log onto, much less peruse. There were no shiny objects in cellophane packaging or aesthetic items of any kind on display here; these things attracted the darkest of customers.

Jars of various specimens with handwritten labels stacked to the ceiling on the left, and open bins of dried animal parts sat in baskets on the right. Mumtaz stopped short and peered at a label. "Noses?" He looked toward the counter, but no one acknowledged him. Next to the noses, he spied other appendages, such as fingers and toes, separated into drawers by digit... and navels.

Next to the appendages lay a full-grown model of a mummy. "Wow is this real?" he asked, leaning in for a closer look. Mumtaz grimaced. The label affixed to it claimed the hair still grew. He had to admit, it looked soft and glossy under the light. His hand reached out to stroke it.

"Please don't touch the hair," Lebe said. Mumtaz jumped at the sound of his voice. He withdrew his hand from it and moved on to the next display. Damn creep.

"Everything is in order," Lebe said, stamping the paper. "We'll need you to sign a waiver, of course," he said, handing it back to Monet. "The liability is yours once it leaves our property, and The Order will not cover any damages."

"That's not a problem," Monet said, stuffing the paper into her purse.

Lebe smirked and produced a scrolled piece of weathered paper with a red ribbon, held in place by a wax seal. He broke the seal and unrolled the antique document, smoothing it flat on the counter.

"Do you know what this is?" he asked Monet.

"Yup," she said, half-listening as she applied gloss to her lips.

"What is it?" Mumtaz had strolled up behind Monet and rested his hand on the small of her back.

"Then I don't have to tell you the consequences if things get out of control, correct?" Lebe asked, ignoring Mumtaz.

"Correct," she said.

"Good. Where will you be storing it?" Lebe asked, producing a fountain pen from somewhere in his strange coat. Mumtaz shivered when Lebe caught him staring.

"What's the address for your warehouse, Taz?" Monet asked.

Mumtaz blinked. "Huh? What for?"

"I need a place to store my merchandise," Monet told him. "Taz is an importer of fine foods," she explained to Lebe. "He's always hunting for exotic items for high-profile chefs," she said. "Maybe you can hook him up with some elephant or zebra," she said.

"Could you do that? Bush meat is hard to come by," Mumtaz said.

"I'm impressed that you would consider such delectable delights," Lebe said, nodding his approval toward Mumtaz.

"Thanks." Lebe's compliments alarmed him, but he found himself flattered that Mo had bragged about his career. *For once.*

"The address?" Lebe asked, uncapping his pen.

"Seventeen eighty-six, Airport Road," Mumtaz said.

"Sign here, please." Lebe turned the parchment around to face him. Hundreds of names scrawled in red ink ran the length of the scroll, each with a line scratched through it. The oldest dates were from the late eighteen hundreds. Several had black smudges next to them. Mumtaz wondered why, but his concern didn't linger.

"Why do I have to sign it?" Mumtaz asked.

"Try to make your handwriting the same size as the others," Lebe said, gesturing for him to take the pen.

"Will this shipment take up a lot of space?" he asked.

"Why? It ain't like you have stuff in there," Monet said.

He sighed and snatched at the pen, but Lebe held fast to it. Mumtaz glowered and challenged the tall man with his stare. A partial flash of a dangerous undercurrent registered in Lebe's intense gaze, and Mumtaz lowered his eyes to the counter. They traveled back up the hideous coat, then further up to Lebe's wide nose, but he dared not look any higher. His mother once told him that eyes were the window to the soul; he certainly didn't want to gaze at Lebe's.

"Same size as the other signatures, please," Lebe said, handing him the pen again. This time, Mumtaz showed respect when he took it from him.

~

LEBE MADE three more phone calls, and forty minutes later, they were on the highway, headed to Rosewood Hollow General Hospital to drop off Monet for her shift.

"Who was that guy? And what are you doing hanging around a place like that? I heard hyenas, Mo, and fucking monkeys. What was that, like Witchmart or something? Oh, you think that's funny? Are you even gonna tell me what I've agreed to store in my warehouse?"

Monet stopped filing her nails and dropped them onto her lap. "Relax, Taz. It's just salt."

Chapter Three

"Mumtaz, you need to step up your game if you expect me to keep buying your products. I could forage my own morels from the forest in my backyard, you know. And you smell like wild animals." Chef Anna Dupree took a long whiff of a wilted mushroom then sat it on top of the others in the crate.

"Yes, Chef." Mumtaz smiled and clasped his hands behind his back. Mumtaz took her threat with a grain of salt. Fat chance she'd find the time to uproot mushrooms. This was the fourth and biggest restaurant she'd opened in the last two years. He knew she got the best deals through him.

The first restaurant, Anna's House, sat in the northwestern part of Rosewood Hollow, near Ashbury Heights. Chef Anna opened a second restaurant in Richmond, near Maymont Park two months later, riding the success of the first. Her third and least successful was in her hometown, New Kent County. Mumtaz had discovered off-track betting during one of his occasional deliveries to the lackluster location, and had been in debt ever since.

Driven by one-upping her culinary rival, Chef Malcolm Perrin, she'd spread herself thin by opening too many restaurants too fast. Sometimes he admired her tenacity. Other times, it made her obnoxious. She reminded him of himself.

"What goodies do you have on the horizon, Mumtaz?"

"Chef?"

"Don't play coy, sir. I'm going broke opening these restaurants. I need you to bring me something good; let's knock the socks off my critics. What have you got on the horizon?"

"I might have some tricks up my sleeve soon, Chef. Give me a couple of days and I'll let you know for sure."

"That's what I want to hear," she said. "I get first dibs, right?"

"Of course, Chef. You're my number one customer." He noticed the sag of dark skin under her eyes as her straw-colored dreads shifted across her prominent forehead when she nodded in satisfaction. Now that she'd spread herself so thin, the overhead was keeping her up at night.

In the past, Mumtaz had been her knight in shining armor. He'd introduced her to an Azerbaijani entrepreneur to taste beluga sturgeon once. The next time, he'd made a name for himself by providing impossible to find Yonezawa beef and black watermelon he'd found through a contact at a poker game. He'd since burned those bridges and found it hard to recoup and rub elbows with the elite players in the culinary world.

Now that he'd gone broke, he didn't have exotic merchandise on hand, nor suppliers on the horizon. The pressure was on, and his reputation was fleeting. He'd never maintain his status by nickel and diming his way in fine foods commerce.

Still, he owed her a great debt. Chef Anna was determined to see a young Black male succeed in an industry where connections were everything. In the beginning, he had been more hood than cosmopolitan, and that had bothered her to no end. She taught him how to refine his code switching and advised him on updating his wardrobe without robbing him of his dignity.

He soaked up what information he could from her, then applied his street sense when applicable. Overall, it was his keen sense of loyalty that helped her grow accustomed to him. Chef Anna loved the way he revered her.

He offered her his best stock. Chef Malcolm got the leftovers, though it wasn't because she paid better, but rather, out of gratitude for Chef Anna. She gave him a chance to grow as an independent businessman in a cutthroat industry, appreciating his unconventional connections and willingness to get any item she asked for.

"Come with me to my office, Mumtaz, I'll pay you for these six crates," she said, separating the ones she wanted from Chef Malcolm's secondhand picks. She dusted her hands on her apron and pivoted on the heels of her black Crocs.

"Yes, Chef," Mumtaz said, falling in line behind the small woman. He prayed never to burn this bridge.

They meandered through the kitchen, past painters and cabinetry installers preparing for the grand opening next Tuesday. The noise from drilling and hammering echoed off the shiny stainless-steel cabinetry.

"Check this out," Chef Anna said with a gleam in her dark brown eyes. Mumtaz watched her red lips part, spreading a proud grin as she pointed to a small nook carved into a wall next to the break room. "This is our butchering room. There's nothing like this in the entire city. Everyone else has to order their beef already cut, but we have full cows coming in this week. Chef Tomás can't wait to get his hands on them, Mumtaz."

"That's great," Mumtaz said, feigning interest. He hoped they weren't about to wax poetic about kitchen gadgetry. They'd already caught him up to speed on the proper knives to use and the most valuable tools around the prep station. He couldn't boil water, so why would he care?

Beady-eyed Chef Tomás looked up from a giant slab of meat laid out on the stainless-steel table before him and stared at Mumtaz. The overpowering, raw smell of the animal parts sickened him. Blood escaped the carcass and traveled across the slanted floor into a drain at the chef's feet. In his bloody apron, holding the butcher knife at the ready, he looked like a maniac.

Chef Tomás lowered his eyes and hacked at the ribs. The separation of skin and bone made Mumtaz uneasy. The act seemed so violent. He wasn't a vegetarian, but he left the dirty work to men with a stomach for it.

A faint memory popped into his head, and he forced it down. Mumtaz swallowed and chased his saliva with a deep breath, but Chef Tomás's precise chops forced it to break the surface. He teleported back in time to the hot and miserable cab of his father's pickup truck.

He was seven years old. The three-hour drive into the desert brought him and his father to an oasis with a sheep farm. It smelled just like this room.

Thanks to his father's good fortune, their household and those of their extended families agreed to share ten slaughtered sheep. His father took him along to make a man of him. Mumtaz didn't realize the defining milestone of manhood was taking life in a slaughterhouse.

He helped, but mostly gagged, and watched his father invoke the name of the Lord as he cut the jugular veins of the sheep before dividing the meat. Everyone, including uncles, aunts, cousins, and siblings, waited back home with bated breath for their bundled package.

Mumtaz's head swam in the heat as blood streamed down the hot sand. On the ride home, he spoke very little, not wanting the stink of the animals to fill his mouth. Upon arriving, he distributed the portions to relatives and realized his mistake. He'd forgotten the head; his father's favorite piece. Their sole portion.

Although the family ate their meatless Eid feast on the first night of celebrations without complaint, Mumtaz burned with shame. His mother, patient and forgiving, made a delicious Tiga dégué, a rice and vegetable dish with peanut sauce that they had frequently. In the late evening, while the others slept, he packed his best traveling clothes and ample water. No one saw him set out on foot across the desert.

Mumtaz retrieved the head from the butcher all by himself and turned for home. A caravan traveling from Bamako found him, and he made it in time for the third day's feast. He arrived at his house; it was full of relatives, newly returned from a burial. News that his father dropped dead on the morning of Mumtaz's lone journey into the desert from a heart attack and worry left him inconsolable. He didn't eat for three weeks.

"Earth to Mumtaz!" Chef Anna said, bringing him back from his daydream.

"I'm sorry Chef, what did you say?"

"I said, I hope you find something delectable this week, Mumtaz. It's been a while since I've had any exotic recipes to try. I'd love to throw something extra special on the menu board during our grand opening," she said. "I'm hoping for another Michelin Star this year."

"I understand," Mumtaz said. "My cousin in Mali may have some thing good for you in a couple of weeks."

"A couple of weeks? That won't do, Mumtaz. I need something now. Why don't you see if you can find some unicorns?"

He scrunched his face. "Unicorns, Chef?"

She snapped her fingers, trying to recall. "It's one of those desert animals. Don't you know some Arabs who can send you some?"

Mumtaz tried to figure out what the hell she meant. He got his phone out and searched for 'Arab unicorn.' "Oh, is this what you're talking about?" He turned the phone and showed her the screen.

"Arabian oryx. That has two horns, Mumtaz, a unicorn has one. Still, I guess Tomás can cut one of them off. Yes, get me one of those."

"I don't think I can, Chef. It's a protected species."

"Mumtaz, I don't want to hear it. If you can get Yonezawa beef, you can get unicorns. Now, let me pay you."

His shoulders slumped. "Yes, Chef." He followed her into her new office, careful not to knock over the stacks of unopened boxes as they made their way to the massive wooden desk in the center of the room.

"Maybe I can get you something good," he said, thinking about the oddities he saw, heard, and smelled in the warehouse at White Crow Shipping. Maybe that creepy dude, Lebe, would turn him on to something strange that Chef Anna could throw on top of some foie gras. "I've got a new contact with some far-out stuff for sale."

"Oh? What is it?" She reached into her blue leather tote bag and pulled out a matching bank deposit bag, then handed him several bills. Mumtaz shoved it in his pocket without counting it.

"I'm not exactly sure what's available yet. My contact is sending me something extra special. I'll call him and find out what goodies he's got," Mumtaz said, leaning towards Chef Anna and winking.

Her eyes lit up. "Ooh, you wanna be like that, huh? Fine, Mumtaz, keep your secrets. As long as you remember me before you think of Chef Malcolm Perrin, I ain't asking too many questions." She ribbed him with an elbow and laughed, full and proud, revealing her gap.

"Always, Chef Anna. And thank you," he said, patting his pocket.

"You're welcome, baby. By the way, what's wrong with your hand? You haven't left it alone since you entered the kitchen."

"I don't know. It looks like the lines are fading, doesn't it?" He showed her his palm.

She peered at it and shook her head. "I don't know what's up with that, Mumtaz. Maybe it's vitiligo. Some areas fade and others don't. Like Michael Jackson."

"I'll look into that," he said. She could be right. The pigment had faded, making his palm look odd. But the grooves of the line itself had faded, too. Vitiligo didn't explain that, but it was the best explanation so far. He excused himself and headed through the kitchen towards the exit.

A box of salt lay on its side, the contents spilling across the counter. Mumtaz pinched a bit of it and threw it over his shoulder like he'd seen in the movies. He didn't believe in all that mumbo jumbo like Mo did, but Allah forgive him, he'd rather be safe than sorry.

Chapter Four

"Are you out of your mind, woman? You're the one who told me to put the account in your name... you can't do this to me. I need the money for my business. There are shipments coming from Mali... Abdullah is sending it... don't you dare close that account... I'll pay you back when the product arrives, and I move it."

Mumtaz wiped the sweat from his brow and neck before it settled on the stiff collar of his white shirt. As the voice droned on in his ear, his shoulders bowed and sent his head nodding into the steering wheel. A soft toot from the horn jerked him awake.

He balled up the sweat-soaked pink and black napkins from Josephine's Bakery in his fist and tossed them into the console's cup holder with the others. The dashboard's clock read half past ten.

Mumtaz sighed at the fireball in the sky beating down on him through the windshield. He balanced the phone on his lap and turned on the speaker as he peeled off his camel suit jacket and white shirt. After all the effort, he found that sitting in his undershirt made no difference.

Spring was feeling a lot like summer these days. The sun was killing him. He glanced at the morels wilting in the backseat. God help him if he lost the entire batch.

"Listen, you owe me money. I'm not letting you renege on our agreement," he said. "What? I'm just like my father. You keep his name out of your mouth. I'm through talking with you. No way. Goodbye. Adios. As Salaamu Alaikum, Mama. I'll see you tonight at dinner."

Mumtaz tossed his cellphone onto the passenger seat. Everybody wanted what he couldn't give them. Money. He punched the ceiling of the twelve-year-old Celica until the stapled upholstery tore loose and draped across his head.

"Unbelievable," he said, ripping out the fabric and throwing it onto the seat next to his phone. Abusing the vehicle felt good. He reached up and pulled down another strip until he had exposed a jagged oval shape of orangish-yellow foam on the driver's side. "That takes care of that," he said, feeling better. He sat back and affixed his eyes on the windshield. The expired inspection sticker robbed him of his satisfaction.

He imagined his mechanic must eat lobster and steak whenever he needed an inspection. According to Hollow Hydraulics, every mechanism under the hood needed immediate servicing, especially the expensive stuff. Mumtaz sighed and started up the car on the third try. Warm air from the vents reminded him he needed antifreeze and an oil change, too.

When he met Monet, he'd been driving a brand-new BMW. Sleek and powerful, the vehicle mirrored who he was at the time. Then his business took a massive hit, and he sold it, downgrading to this pile of rubbish.

One of these days, he would drive to the car crushers on Bradlee Street and squeeze the life out of this derelict piece of shit. Then, he'd watch the little cube fade away in the rearview mirror of his brand-new Cadillac. One day soon. He settled back in the seat, letting warm air push the beads of sweat around his forehead.

Mumtaz took a deep breath and tried to picture a new car. Manifestation. Mo spent her downtime watching new-age channels on Vewz, always running a show in the background. It seemed corny, but what the hell?

He wasn't sure, but he could almost see something if he shut his eyes hard enough. 'Picture the future and what you want.' *Money. And lots of it.* 'Dream your life. Set up a vision board,' the flaky-looking woman on the t.v. had said.

He thought about living in a cottage on the islands near Calliope Falls, just like Mo wanted. Mumtaz pushed his lids together as tight as they would go, then let out the breath he'd been holding. Breathe. Let the future come to you.

"The future," he mouthed. He couldn't tell if it was the future, but he saw something. A flash of light, like a bang or explosion. That must be me crossing the threshold, he reasoned. "Becoming a rich mother-fucker," he said into the warm air blowing from the vent.

The idea of wealth brought a smile to Mumtaz's lips. All those smug assholes from the hood and those gold-digging chicken heads would change their tunes when they saw him and his mother rolling through the neighborhood for the last time, moving truck in tow. The people who lived near his mother clowned him when he'd lost his newly earned fortune, but not this time. This time, they'd really move out of there.

Forget moving their old things. His mother deserved new things, and a new house in the bougie part of town. Copperhead Cliffs. He'd buy her those designer handbags and perfumes she wanted from Valley Mall, too. He'd stop borrowing money from her. Instead, she'd take an allowance from him, and he wouldn't have to hear about how his older sister was a better child than he.

There was just one thing. His mother wanted him to marry a girl from back home. He despised all the local Malians' too-westernized daughters. If he were going to marry someone who was from here, he might as well get the real thing.

Could he get her to accept Mo as his wife? Of course he could; Mo would have to cut out the witchy woo-woo stuff in front of his family. She could do whatever she liked in the privacy of their bedroom, but he wasn't having it in front of his mom. Over time, Mo would wise up and change. Women always behaved when you gave them a little money.

The phone rang, bringing him back to life. Mumtaz groaned and reached over to retrieve it from the seat. "Talk fast. I'm running out of minutes."

"With your broke ass," the caller said.

Mumtaz grinned. "Jazzy Jasim, what's up, homie?" Besides himself, Jasim Diallo was the one person in the world Mumtaz could count on when he was in a bind. Maybe they were tight like they were because Jasim never let him borrow money. He said he didn't want it to come between them.

"I'm not doing much. I've got the day off, and Nyah's mother is here at our house. Swing by and pick me up, please."

"Bet. Give me about ten minutes. You can come with me to unload this produce," Mumtaz said, wincing at the crates of rubbery mushrooms in the rearview mirror. It hurt him to see the formerly beautiful fungi in such a state. He'd saved up and paid a Maryland farmer to forage on his land for two hours. There had been so many good ones, all he had to do was pluck them out of the earth.

He didn't do it himself, of course. Four meth heads from the hood agreed to fill up the crates for twenty dollars apiece. Addicts will work hard and fast when they're hungry for a fix.

The sun cut his expected profit by eight hundred dollars so far. Fucking global warming. A pretty boy in a black and red Bugatti approached, and Mumtaz gave the driver the side eye as he sped by. Rich motherfuckers like that hid in their penthouse suites and yachts while he suffered in the elements.

"The sooner you pick me up, the better, Taz. All the women in this house are crazier than me today."

"You got it, Jasim. Wait outside for me." They hung up, and Mumtaz tossed the phone onto the seat once more and drove out of the parking lot.

Mumtaz met 'Jazzy' Jasim Diallo at Edgewater Junior High School. The connection between the two West African boys of single mothers was instant. They'd spent every moment together since then, except in the past year. Jasim married a girl Mumtaz hadn't heard a thing about until the deed was done. It stung when he found out.

Jasim treated Mumtaz to a burger combo with a strawberry shake at Syreeta's when he returned from his honeymoon on a Disney cruise to soften the blow. "Taz, it's time to grow up. We're almost thirty. Don't you want to settle down too?"

How could his best friend do something so permanent without consulting him first? He'd let Jasim in on every important detail of his life, like when he bought a used washer for his mother. Wasn't this at least as big as that?

"You don't even know the girl," Mumtaz had said.

"I sure know, Naya now. Inside and out," Jasim said, ribbing Mumtaz with an elbow.

Mumtaz sipped his shake and stared into space. "I can't believe you got married to a ho that you knew for six hours."

Jasim dropped his burger on his plate and leaned in close. "Damn, Taz, that's my wife you're talking about. The queen of my house, mother of my future-born jazz aficionados. She ain't a ho. She's a good Muslim woman, and we could both benefit from her presence. Now apologize before I kick your little disrespectful ass."

"Sorry. I didn't mean to insult you like that. I'm just in shock. You're the guy who gets women to throw their thongs on the stage in a jazz cafe in the basement of a damn pastry shop. You ain't even the lead singer. I don't understand why you'd swap that for the ball and chain."

"You should meet her. I think you two would get along." Jasim leaned forward. "She works at your favorite cargo company."

Mumtaz sat up straighter. "Royal Egyptian?"

"That's right. You're looking at deep discounts in your future, Taz. We're talking thirty-five percent."

"She can do that?"

"She sure can. Once Nyah starts saving you some money, you can put it back into your business."

Mumtaz rubbed his chin and a smile spread across his face as he crunched numbers in his head. "That's what I'm talking about, Jasim. I might have some use for her after all."

"'Some use for her?' Taz, if I hadn't known you my entire life, I'd knock your teeth down your throat."

"Hold that thought. I need to check something out." He scrolled through the menu of the off-track betting venue and placed his wager.

Jasim shook his head.

"Sorry about that. Had some business. Now, I'm still trying to figure out why you'd mess up the good thing we had by marrying this chick," Mumtaz said. He cringed at the sound of his own sulking voice.

"Man, you sound like a jealous female."

"Whatever. If you want to discover her skeletons a little at a time, who am I to criticize?"

"Why can't you be happy for me and hope for the best? She's got me praying again. I got a new job. I'm sober. Hell, I don't even smoke weed anymore."

Mumtaz shrugged. "More for me and Mo."

"Change your mindset, Taz. When one of us rises, the other one does too."

"That's funny, Jasim, because from where I'm standing, you're the only one going up," Mumtaz said, biting on his straw.

"You sound positively green, my friend."

Mumtaz turned his pockets inside out. "I don't see my bank account getting fat like yours, and there's definitely no woman warming my bed."

"What about Mo?"

"Romps in the hay and Mo throwing me out before I can get my boxers on, don't count... Mo's not barefoot and pregnant, waiting on me with a hot meal and a drink after a long day. Not yet anyway."

"Yep. Jealous. Let me hear you say it, Taz."

"Say what?"

"Man, stop playing. Say MashaAllah, so I don't get the evil eye."

Mumtaz sucked his teeth. "Fine, whatever, Negro. MashaAllah, may Allah give you more."

"Ameen," Jasim said, biting into his burger with a satisfied smile. The waitress sat the check on the corner of the table.

"And may He give you the money for the check," Mumtaz said, tossing the bill at his friend.

"InshaAllah," Jasim said, cracking a smile.

Thinking about it now, Mumtaz didn't believe it was jealousy. He just hated how things worked out for Jasim for no reason. He played the upright bass for a living; how could he afford such a beautiful home in Hillstead Village? It made little sense.

For Mumtaz, everything turned from gold to shit. Reversed Midas Touch. From his car wash venture, to a stint with a coin laundry, it all went belly up. Didn't people need to wash their funky clothes anymore?

He couldn't shake the family curse. His mother hated when he brought it up. Its darkness clung to him.

The inner workings of his mind surprised him. He glanced at

himself in the rearview mirror, wondering what his father would say. *You're lost.*

As Mumtaz turned into the neighborhood, he snapped out of it in time to see Jasim standing on the corner of his street, three doors down from his house, with a backpack slung on one shoulder. When Jasim carried a bag, it meant he wasn't sure if he should come home late that night or the next morning. Nyah might let him in when he got home, and she might not.

"As Salaamu Alaikum. Trouble in paradise?" Mumtaz asked. When Jasim's wife got mad, Mumtaz somehow got Jasim into more trouble. He smiled, giddy from the potential troubles they could get into in the foreseeable future.

"Wa Alaikum As Salaam. Just a tiff," Jasim said, shutting the passenger door.

"Uh huh. That's why you've got your toothbrush and a pair of boxers in your bag, right?"

"Yeah, whatever, Taz. So, what are you selling today?" Jasim turned around to inspect the crates. "What are those? And why do they smell like that?"

"A nuisance. You know that farmer I told you about? He let me pick up these morels two days ago. My AC gave out on the way back from Maryland, and this batch couldn't handle the heat. I sold the good ones yesterday, and I stored the rest in my mom's fridge last night. This was supposed to be an easy sale."

"One step forward, two steps back," Jasim said. "Same old sad song, Taz."

"I know, right? I've gotta catch a break or my importer days are over."

"What are you planning to do with those?" Jasim nodded towards the back seat.

"Sell them."

"Well, whatever you need, homie, I'm here for you."

"What I need is money."

"What I'm gonna give you is my moral support," Jasim said.

Mumtaz rolled his eyes. "Thanks, Jasim. That's gonna really help me beat this thing."

"What thing? Your knack for making poor decisions? I told you to buy that refrigerated truck when you had the chance. It was a steal."

Mumtaz gritted his teeth in silence, swallowing the degradation. Jasim had been right about the truck. Right about everything. That's why he didn't bother mentioning the extreme amount of debt hanging over his head after the horse races. Hearing 'I told you so,' would put him over the edge. "Maybe the truck is still available. I'll look into it next week."

"Nope. I checked last night, and the truck is gone. Somebody bought it right under your nose. You gotta start following my advice, Taz. Otherwise, you're gonna keep suffering from your... weird situation."

"It's okay to call it what it is. My curse. I'm suffering from my curse."

"I don't know about all that, but either way, I'm still down for you, homie."

Mumtaz made a right onto Yukiko Street in Hillstead Village and parked on the street. He and Jasim fished the crates of morels out of the back seat and tossed them onto a dolly he kept lodged in the trunk.

"In ten minutes, I'm going to convince someone to buy all three crates of morels and give a finger to the curse."

"That's right, Taz. Fuck that curse." Jasim extended his hand, and the two slapped palms. "Then invest in your business. Buy a new truck."

"You're right. I will." Mumtaz stacked the final crate onto the dolly. It was time to turn things around. If he didn't, Lord help him.

Chapter Five

"WHAT THE HELL is this crap, Taz? These mushrooms look like the erasers that Antoine bites off the server pencils." Rosie Sann, the rodent-faced sous chef at Brimstone's Grille, who had no authority to purchase anything for the restaurant, and therefore, Mumtaz didn't give a damn about, scrunched her nose at his crates of morels.

"Rosie's right, Taz. Why are you always trying to peddle junk at us, man? We throw out food in better condition than this." Saucier, and constant thorn in Mumtaz's side, Tampa Valentine, took the lead from Rosie and inspected the produce. When he finished sticking his nose where it didn't belong, he stepped aside for his senior chef, Eduardo King, the actual decision-maker.

"What do you think, Eddie? Can you salvage enough of these to pay me what I'm asking for?" Mumtaz nodded at Eduardo, hoping he'd remember the occasions when he was the guy they called for rare ingredients in the eleventh hour. Captive-raised Burchell zebra meat is scarce. Mumtaz kicked himself for losing favor with his Kenyan contacts.

"It's a no, from me, Taz. My daughter's play food looks better than this crap." Eduardo shoved the box at Mumtaz, while Rosie and Tampa hid their snickers.

"Come on, guys. I'm asking for a favor. I could pick through them and give you the best ones for seven-fifty." Thank God he'd left Jasim outside. He'd rather die than have his friend witness his begging.

"I hope you mean seven dollars and fifty cents," Rosie said, tossing a tea towel over her shoulder and walking away. Tampa shook his head and went to the walk-in freezer. If only he could figure out when those two took an actual lunch break, he could get Eduardo alone and lean into him. His game wasn't so confident with those two loud-mouths around.

"Eduardo, please. I need this right now. I sold the rest to Chef Anna this morning. She didn't need the rest."

Eduardo raised an eyebrow. "Anna from Dupree Steakhouse?"

Mumtaz gave himself a mental kick in the ass for mentioning her name. "Yeah," he muttered.

"For crying out loud, Taz. She's our direct competition. She buys up all the quality ingredients, even if she doesn't need them. Do you know what she does with the excess, Taz? She donates it to homeless shelters to spite us."

"I may have heard something about that," Mumtaz said, looking sheepish.

"So, you went bright and early to Chef Anna Dupree's place and sold her quality morels, then brought your shriveled rejects to us?" Chef Eduardo snapped to attention, and Mumtaz turned to face Executive Chef and owner of Brimstone's, Malcolm Perrin. He stood with his arms folded, overlooking the scene from the doorway of the break room.

Mumtaz started a little. *How long has he been standing there?* Looking like that detective in the Dashiell Hammett book with the devilish beard and mustache, the chef waited for an answer.

Appearance aside, Chef Malcolm was a good man, and his business was steaks. He rarely succumbed to overspending and never partook in indulgences like the other chefs did. If they wanted to shorten their lifespans by doing lines of coke in the alley that was fine by him, but it had better not be during prep or dinner service. He ran a tight ship, and if they didn't like it, they could go cook soul fusion or whatever the heck Anna Dupree claimed to make.

Despite the morels resembling dried sea sponges, Mumtaz approached Chef Malcolm with his meager offering. The chef looked pissed already; there was nothing to lose.

"My intention was to bring them here earlier, but you guys were in a meeting all morning, Chef. I'm sorry," Mumtaz said. Chef Malcolm sighed. "It has been unseasonably hot. Come on, player, er Chef. Isn't there anything you can do?"

Chef Malcolm stroked his beard as his eyes bore into Mumtaz's. He hoped the man would take pity on him. If he did, maybe Mumtaz might come to him first with something from his next big-ticket item. Maybe.

"I'm going to pass this time, Mumtaz."

Damn. The overdue bills stacked up in the glove box of his car popped into his head. "I'll take three-fifty," Mumtaz offered.

Chef Malcolm started walking away. "Bring me something palatable, and we'll talk."

"Wait Chef—Chef, how about two-fifty? A hundred? Spot me a hundred... we can consider it an advance on the next delivery. I have something good coming in, I swear!"

Chef Malcolm stopped walking. "I said no, Mumtaz. Maybe next time. And I swear to you, on my mother's grave, if you ever bring something like this to my restaurant again, you won't do business anywhere on the east coast, understand? Now, have some dignity and stop begging. Get your shit together."

Warmth spread across his dark brown cheeks. "Yes, Chef." Mumtaz gathered the crates onto the dolly.

He wheeled the rejected morels into the alley behind Brimstone's and glanced at the back door of the new restaurant across the narrow cobblestone road, Andalusia. *Don't do this to her. She's family, you asshole.* His conscience told him to dump the crates into the garbage bin and call it a loss, but he rarely listened to his inner voice. Why start today?

He heard Eduardo and crew horsing around in the kitchen behind him and shrank into himself. They were laughing at him, he knew it. The way they talked down to him hurt his ego and pissed him off because he couldn't do a damn thing about it.

I can't let the morels go to waste; I've got to try. Some money was better than no money, and she would give it to him, even if she didn't want them. He tucked his tail between his legs and approached the back door of Andalusia. Somewhere, the one who'd cursed him was having a good laugh.

"Excuse me, can you get the door? I'd like to talk to Aminah," he said to the two chefs leaning against the brick wall, smoking. The taller one nodded and pulled open the door for him. "Thanks, man." Mumtaz sighed and entered his cousin's new establishment.

～

"Why didn't you come to me in the first place? I would have purchased all of your mushrooms, Mumtaz." Aminah pushed back a layer of dried mushrooms from the top crate, searching for good ones. The corners of her mouth turned upward, and a hand flew to her lips. He appreciated that she tried to hide it.

"As you can see, Aminah, they aren't that great." Mumtaz wrinkled his forehead and looked into the gentle brown eyes of his baby cousin. Her smile reached them, and she shook her head at him in mock exasperation. He hated himself for this.

"Mumtaz, Mumtaz, Mumtaz. Come with me." She invited him into her office—even cutting short an appointment with her best friend, Haleema, for him to showcase his product. As she inspected the mushrooms, Mumtaz tugged at his collar and fought the urge to thank her for her time and leave. Aminah was the best.

He hoped word didn't get back to his mother. Even if it was first-class produce, she'd complain about Aminah bailing him out. Again.

"It was nice to see Haleema, brief as it was," Mumtaz said. "I see she started wearing the hijab." Aminah and Haleema had been in the middle of a photo shoot for Aminah's new menu, but she packed up in a hurry and left before he could talk to her. He'd always liked Haleema. Always wanted her for himself. But she liked white guys.

"She's been wearing a hijab for two years, Mumtaz," Aminah said, picking through the mushrooms again.

"Oh, I didn't realize. It looks good on her. Not that she wasn't attractive before—"

"Ahem," Aminah said, shooting him a stern look. "My friend doesn't need that kind of attention from you right now, Mumtaz. Let her live her life."

"I'm just saying how lovely she looks, Aminah. That's not a sin, is it?"

Aminah shook her head and dove back into the mushrooms.

"So, is Haleema still seeing that guy? What's his name? Arthur?"

"Andrew, and no, she's not."

"That's great." Aminah shot her cousin a quizzical look. "What I mean to say is that I hope she finds someone better, InshaAllah." If things didn't work out with Mo, Haleema might be a suitable alternative. She was one of those bad good girls. The kind with a past and a dirty secret. He'd keep her in the back of his mind, just in case.

"Ameen. May she find someone worthy," Aminah said.

"She was in a hurry, though," Mumtaz said. "What was that about?"

"Maybe she wanted to get away from you, cousin."

"Ouch, Aminah. That hurt my feelings," Mumtaz said, clutching his heart.

"I doubt that. Is there any woman you won't chase?"

"There's one, because she's already spoken for. I hope you're not disappointed, cousin."

"I'll try to survive," Aminah said, rolling her eyes. "I'll see you at dinner in a couple of days, right?"

"Sure. Is Reza coming too?"

"No, he's away on business." The smile fell from her face at the mention of her husband. He noticed for the first time how tired she looked.

"That guy is always gone," Mumtaz said. "That's how I want to be."

"Excuse me?" Aminah placed a hand on her hip and waited for clarification.

"I want to be on the go, making deals and growing my business," he explained. "Things are kind of pathetic right now." His shoulders slumped. The pain from his misery hit hard when he said it aloud.

Aminah lay her small brown hand on his shoulder and gave him a gentle squeeze. "Don't worry, cousin, you'll pull through. Now, tell me how much I owe you."

"Forget it, cousin, I'm wasting your time."

"Nonsense. I can soak them in water to revive them. How much?"

"For you? Fifty bucks," he said.

Aminah frowned. "Just fifty? Don't be shy, Mumtaz. Tell me, how much were you expecting from Malcolm?"

He opened his mouth, ready to say she was his first choice, and closed it. He couldn't lie to her. "I hate how you're too nice, Aminah. It makes me think that somebody's gonna hurt you one day. Don't worry about me, okay? Fifty dollars is good enough."

"I'm going to give you four hundred."

"Aminah—"

"Don't you dare protest, Mumtaz. We're family. Families help each other."

"I don't want you to spend too much, cousin. I know things are tight right now with this new restaurant. Congratulations, by the way."

"Thank you. And yes, they are tight, but we're doing well, despite the protesters outside."

"Protesters?"

"In front of the restaurant," she said, thumbing through bills she pulled from a cash box buried inside her messy desk drawer. The crease in her forehead betrayed her calm demeanor.

"What are they protesting?"

"This and that," she said, as she unwrapped a stack of twenty-dollar bills. "People don't want me serving halal meat. Some don't want me serving meat at all."

"Why don't they protest at the steakhouse behind you?" Mumtaz asked, thumbing towards Brimstone's.

"I think we know why," Aminah said, tugging at her hijab.

"It's the damn curse," Mumtaz said, frowning. "It's coming for you, too."

Aminah stopped counting and shot her cousin a puzzled glance. "Are you serious? Have you been talking to our cousins in Mali?" Mumtaz shrugged and remained quiet. "That's your problem right there. Abdullah and his notions. He's conducting his own witch hunt. Do you know the authorities have threatened to put him in prison if he keeps bothering everybody?"

"I don't understand why they don't take him seriously."

"I'll tell you why," Aminah said. "He's spreading fear and superstition. He thinks some crazy person put a curse on our family and drove us out of the country, away from our people and our homes. And here you are, bringing up that mess in America."

"Admit it. Things don't turn out well for me," Mumtaz said.

"Be wise about your money and make better decisions, cousin. Until you do, your life will remain the chaos that it is. Here's your four hundred dollars. Kiss Auntie for me when you get home."

~

"Look what I got," Mumtaz sang as he jogged toward his old Toyota, fanning the four hundred dollars his cousin had given him. Jasim sat on the hood of the car, reading a chick-lit book. If Mumtaz wasn't so hyped, he might have teased him about it.

"My man, you came through," he said, cracking a smile and shooting him a thumbs up. He looked past Mumtaz's shoulder and paused, hand frozen in mid-air. "Aw, shit." Jasim scrambled off the hood of the car, putting distance between himself and whatever was behind Mumtaz. Had he been paying attention, he would have avoided the awaiting sucker punch.

"Jasim!" Mumtaz started as he watched his friend hit the pavement. Someone behind Mumtaz snatched the money from his raised hands.

"Hey!" Mumtaz turned to look, then froze.

"Good work. This should cover the lunch bill for me and the boys. Now, where's the rest of the money that you owe me?" A grim-faced man with a short black beard fanned out the bills in his hand, then handed them to a man in a shark-skin suit.

"Luqman. I can explain." Mumtaz took a deep breath and sneaked a look at the palm of his hand. Had the line shrunk again, or was it his imagination?

Chapter Six

"I LIKE it when people come to me for help. It means two things. Number one, my reputation precedes me; people realize they can count on me to help them out of sticky situations. Like Robin Hood. And number two, because of my reputation, they know that if they cross me, there's no one who can save them. Mumtaz, I feel like you don't know my reputation. Why else would you cross me like this?"

Mumtaz and Jasim watched Luqman Rahmaninov toss a pair of dice on the table and snatch them up over and over with a deft swipe of his fingers. They landed on seven each time. He swiped them from the table a final time and began pacing like a hungry tiger in front of them.

Mumtaz took solace that his thugs didn't tie them to the chairs. They were in Nouman's, an Indo-Arab fusion restaurant three blocks away from Andalusia. Luqman allowed them to remain sitting, like ordinary gentlemen, hands flat on the table, pockets emptied.

Mumtaz kept one eye on the stalking Luqman, and another on the two guys stationed at the empty restaurant's door. Their presence made this anything but an ordinary business meeting. The message was loud and clear.

"From the looks of that ugly-ass jacket and your beat down Toyota, you haven't been on a shopping spree in a long time. So, what are you doing with my money, Taz?"

"I need a little more time, Luke. A couple of deals fell through and—" Mumtaz looked up from the floor into Luqman's expressionless eyes and quit talking. If he had been in one of his moods, tossing tables and breaking glasses, Mumtaz could take it. Angry Luqman was consolable. Stare into your soul Luqman was scary.

Mumtaz held Luqman in a higher esteem than the other loan sharks in town because they shared the same faith. Neither one of them was any good at it, but he respected a man who flew the same banner. But Luqman was a two-bit crook, and like the rest of the bookies and loan sharks, if Mumtaz screwed up, there was no reprieve from Luqman's blade cutting his throat.

"You always have an excuse, don't you, Taz? Let's see, you couldn't pay me back because the builder for your warehouse was shady and overcharged you. Your mom needed crowns on her teeth. Your car broke down. Twice. You paid for your friend Jasim's honeymoon, and he asked to borrow some money from you to take his wife on a vacation during the holidays, blah, blah. So many excuses. What is it this time, Taz?"

Mumtaz felt the heat from Jasim's eyes on his cheek. He was going to get an earful of bitching and complaining later.

"The curse is getting more powerful," Mumtaz said.

Luqman's eyebrows shot up in confusion for a moment as he locked eyes with Mumtaz. "My God," he said. He backed off, then smiled and ran a hand through his loose black curls. "Not the goddamned curse stuff again. Taz, look at me. Baby, you've got to let that shit go. Superstitious nonsense like that holds you back. I'm from Chechnya. Do you know how many folktales we hear from the old women? You can't take it to heart, my friend."

Luqman approached Mumtaz and slapped him across the cheek hard enough to draw blood with the ring on his pinky finger. He'd learned how to backhand just so, leaving the impression of the star and crescent. He blasphemed, calling it 'The seal of the profit.'

"I want my money by the end of the week, or you're gonna be on my list of to-dos. Oh, and Jasim's gonna lose three fingers on each hand." Luqman twisted the ring on his finger three times and kissed it. "As Salaamu Alaikum, Taz. Saturday night, I will come looking for you and Jasim. Then I will let you watch me slice off his fingers. By the way, Jasim, I caught your show the other night at Josephine's. You play one hell of an upright bass. Chef's kiss," he said, kissing his thumb and first two fingers.

～

"MOTHERFUCKING LUCKY LUKE? What was that, Taz? You've been lying to a gangster about money?"

"What does he care what I use it for? I go to him for a loan, he tells me how much I owe and when. It's really none of his business how I spend the money, or who I give it to."

"Uh huh. And who exactly did you give it to, Taz, because it sure as hell wasn't me? You never gave me a dime for my honeymoon or otherwise. This is some bullshit," Jasim said, kicking rocks along the curb as they walked the three blocks back to the car.

"I know, I lied, Jasim, but I needed the money for my business. And I gave a little to Mo. She was short, and I know she's good for it."

"I'm not a part of your business, Taz. I'm your married friend, with a baby on the way." Jasim winced and crouched when they reached an intersection, planting his head between his hands. "I'm about to get sick," he said, holding onto the bottom of a street sign.

Mumtaz sighed. "Wait here." He crossed the street and walked up to the drive-thru window of The Inside Scoop Ice Cream Shoppe. He waved to the girl in the drive-thru window and asked her something. She nodded and disappeared. While he waited, Mumtaz scoured the pavement for loose change. The girl reappeared with a cup and handed it to him. He took the cup, pocketed the change, and returned to Jasim.

"You're unbelievable," Jasim said. "Is pocket change more important than my life?"

"Don't be dramatic, Jasim. Here, drink up. Cindy says hi." Jasim peered at the girl in the window, then waved when he recognized the younger sister of his bandmate, Tony. They'd gone out behind Tony's back when Jasim was single.

"Dramatic? Mumtaz, he wants to cut off my goddamned fingers. I think I have a right to react with a little flair, don't you?" He popped the top off the cup and gulped down the cold Coke.

"I doubt he'd mess up your hands. His beef is with me. If he wanted to kill us, we'd be dead. Luqman is a street hustler from the bottom of the barrel. He ain't gonna kill nobody. He's skittish about lending money for too long because he's trying to build his empire. As long as we get the money to him in time, we're good."

A homeless man with a shopping cart passed by and Jasim placed the change from his pocket into a plastic cup taped to a sign. 'Give money, get money,' his mom always said.

"Don't sell me your fantasies, Taz. I know what Lucky Luke does to people." Jasim ran his finger across the length of his throat.

"You're tripping."

"How much do you owe him, Taz? Like, really owe him?"

"Not much."

"How much is not much?"

"About fifteen or twenty thousand. That's nothing to Luqman."

"Fifteen or twenty thousand?" Jasim's jaw dropped. "My man, that might be chump change to Lucky Luke, but you sure as hell don't have thirty-five thousand dollars."

"I said fifteen or twenty."

"And I know you well enough to add them together. How long have you owed him?"

"A few months."

Jasim folded his arms on his chest and peered at his friend. "What's a few, Taz?"

"Like a year or something."

"A year, huh? And when were you supposed to pay it back?"

"He gave me four months. Oh, come on, Jasim. Don't look at me like that. I needed an extension, and he gave it to me."

"And when did that expire?"

"Six months ago. I paid him eleven grand, but I needed to borrow it again to buy the warehouse. An importer without a warehouse won't make it in the business for long."

"Why do you have to make things hard for everybody, Taz? You have a business degree. Shouldn't you know how to run one?"

"I know how to run a business, Jasim. Success and business sense aren't mutually exclusive."

"Neither is common sense." Jasim finished the coke and replaced the top. He sat on his haunches for a moment longer and thought about the mess his friend had gotten him into. "Your mother must be ashamed. Thank Allah your father can't see what a failure you've become."

"Hey, fuck you, Jasim. You don't have to get personal."

"Personal? I'm a victim of your screw up and I can't take a dig at you? My wife's gonna freak. She told me I need better friends. Maybe I should listen to her; she hasn't failed me yet."

Mumtaz squeezed his hands into a fist. This again. Jasim's chick was a thorn in his side. "Jasim, why are you so soft? Has married life taken away your balls? Life is about taking risks, not marrying the first hot tramp willing to carry you."

Jasim launched himself at Mumtaz, smashing him into a brick wall. He kneed Mumtaz in the crotch and watched him crumpled to the ground, clutching his aching groin.

"What the fuck, Jasim?" Mumtaz rolled onto his side and whimpered as waves of nausea threatened to spill the contents of his stomach all over the pavement.

"Who's crying about their balls now?" A group of girls in a car leaving the ice cream shop blasted the horn and screamed obscenities at them. Jasim backed off, then walked down the street to the ancient Celica. Minutes later, Mumtaz hobbled slowly to the car.

"I'm not soft, Taz. I'm cautious. And I'm the sole breadwinner in my family with a wife and mother-in-law who expect me to put food on the table and keep a roof over their heads. Not to mention, I have to worry about my mother's convalescence."

"No, you're soft, Jasim. You've changed since back in the day. They used to call you 'Hellraiser.' Your nickname doesn't fit you anymore. Look at my clothes. This was my best jacket. You'd better hope this comes out at the cleaners."

"You need to grow up, Taz. I'm a man now, and the days of raising hell are behind us." Jasim opened and closed his hands. "Why the hell does he want to cut off my fingers, anyway? Why not yours?"

"Because it will hurt me more to know that I'm the reason they're gone. He's small-time, but he can be a vindictive bastard. This way, I will never forget my mistake."

Jasim's hands dropped to his side. "Getting your best friend's fingers chopped off is a fucked-up thing to do. You better figure a way out of this mess, Taz. Or I'll use the remaining digits to strangle you."

"Wallahi, I will. I promise," Mumtaz said with his hand on his heart.

Jasim sucked his teeth. "You think taking Allah's name in an oath means something to me? This isn't like that time I got my nose broken in high school because we stole a lemon from that shady car dealership for a joy ride. These are my fingers, Taz. My livelihood. Josephine doesn't employ fingerless musicians, and I can't survive off of disability checks."

"Right, right," Mumtaz said, scrolling through his phone.

"Oh, I'm sorry, am I distracting you?"

"Nope," he said, continuing to scroll. "I met this creep through Mo today. He works at a warehouse near the big cemetery. He's got a lot of crazy shit in there. If he'll let me look through it, I'll see what I can come up with."

He dug in his pocket and found the business card for White Crow Shipping and dialed the number. Lebe's deep voice gave him an immediate case of regret. 'I implore you to leave a message at the beep.' *Implore.* Mumtaz wondered if they dug Lebe out of a time capsule, then left a message, *imploring* him to call back.

When he finished, he hung up the phone and shrugged at his friend. "All we can do now is wait and see," Mumtaz said.

"Wait, and see? You better get back on the phone and start a 'Go Fund Me' page. What if this dude doesn't have any products for you to move?"

Mumtaz dropped his eyes, unable to look at his friend. "I honestly don't know."

〜

"I WANT you to pay the money you owe me for the warehouse and when are you going to do something with your life? Mumtaz!"

"What, Mama?" Mumtaz stared at the palm of his hand, wondering if it was shorter than it had been earlier in the day. He reached for his cellphone, then remembered how strict his mother was about phone calls at dinner. Besides, she hadn't forgiven him for paying the warehouse fees late. She wouldn't have cared if he hadn't put it in her name.

"I don't like eating dinner this late, Mumtaz. It's nine o'clock! What self-respecting man eats dinner this late when his mother spent the whole day cooking for him? Stop staring at your hand and answer me, boy." A bolt of lightning cracked across the evening sky, lighting up the dining room in his mother's two-bedroom bungalow. A rumble of thunder answered, rattling the little figurines in her curio cabinet and the few pieces of China she owned.

"What did you say, Mama?" He rose from the table, ignoring the intricate henna patterns on her extended finger, and opened a drawer in the buffet table.

"I said, when are you getting married and giving me a grandchild? Your cousin, Aminah, is having her second baby."

"No, you didn't," Mumtaz said, rifling in the drawer. "You asked when I was going to do something with my life?"

"Why didn't you answer me in the first place if you heard the question?"

"Because no matter what I say, it won't be the right answer. I could be a multi-millionaire and you would still ask me what I was doing with my life. Ah, here it is," he said, grabbing a black marker from the drawer.

"Mumtaz, if you become a *thousandaire*, I promise never to ask about your life."

Mumtaz cracked a crooked smile. "You promise?" he asked, as he drew a thick, short line from the middle of his ring finger to the receding line in his palm. He'd have to ask Mo if the line had been between his ring finger and pinky the last time she saw it. She probably mentioned it, but he couldn't remember.

"Well, I won't ask about the direction of your life, but I can't make any promises about not asking for grandchildren once in a while."

"Fair enough," he said.

"What are you doing with that marker?"

"Research."

"For what? Don't tell me you're thinking about manufacturing gloves now. Can't you stick to one business venture? I'd be proud if you could see one of your endeavors come to fruition."

"So would I, Mama. Blessings don't seem to come my way, do they?"

"I had a dream about you last night," she said, gathering rice into the middle of her plate with oily fingers.

"Don't talk about nightmares, Mama."

"It wasn't a nightmare, just a strange dream. I think it was a warning. I dreamed about a strange being who traveled across the ocean and spread itself across our town. It started raining, but it wasn't water that fell from the sky. It was salt," she said, staring through him.

Mumtaz drank from his glass of lukewarm water and wished for ice. His mother refused to hook up the ice maker in the fridge or buy ice trays to make it, for fear of ruining their teeth. His mother continued.

"It filled my mouth, and I choked it down, making my belly big and pregnant. The pains came, and I pushed something out of me. Bloody salt crystals stuck to its skin. It had your face." She shuddered.

He sat the glass on the table and stared at her. "What kind of dream is that, Mama? Why did it have my face? Did you make that up?"

His mother shook her head. "You're right. I shouldn't discuss nightmares. Allah, spare us from black magic," she said, mashing rice between her fingers with pieces of tender beef.

"Ameen," Mumtaz said. He pushed away his plate and knocked over the saltshaker. They both stared at the spilled contents. He pinched it like he'd seen people do in the movies and threw a bit over his left shoulder.

"Astaghfirullah, Mumtaz. That's sacrilegious."

"I don't want more bad luck. Better safe than sorry, right?"

"There is no such thing as bad luck." She glowered. "Trusting Allah is better than burning in the Hellfire."

"Okay, Mama, you're right." He held up his hands, surrendering.

His mother glowered at him, then flicked the rice and meat from her fingers back into the plate. "Don't be late for dinner on Friday night, okay? It's bad luck to ruin your guests' good time."

Mumtaz raised an eyebrow at her, but kept his mouth shut. "Yes, Mama."

"Maybe Aminah knows a good girl that you can marry. I'll ask her when she and her sisters get here."

"I'm sure you will." His cellphone buzzed in his pocket. They both sat there, waiting.

"Go on and answer it, Mumtaz. Don't complain about your hunger later."

"Thank you, Mama." He missed the call, but a short text followed. *Saturday night or else. -Luke.* The text caught him off guard, but he didn't have time to fret over it. He checked the one remaining voicemail from Mo and left the table.

Chapter Seven

"Thanks for coming to pick me up, Taz. I'm soaked to the bone," Mo said, pulling wet strands of hair from the corner of her mouth. "I'll be so glad when I get a new car. I'm manifesting every day. It's gonna be so beautiful. You don't know how hard it is being a nurse on call without a car, even for a day or two."

"You're welcome, Mo. Why don't you rent one?" Mumtaz laid a clean blanket from the trunk of his Celica across Mo's lap and turned the dial on the temperature control to the warmest fan setting that wouldn't fog up the windows. The storm raged around them in the parking lot of the after-hours care clinic near the hospital.

"Too expensive. I did one of your moves and put all the money I had into my product."

Mumtaz shook his head. "You're broke? I can't believe you spent so much money on salt. Please tell me that you don't have cash problems because of this. Mo, it's salt."

"You don't have to be a dick about it, Taz. I needed some of it for rent, and the rest is going to make a killing for me. Do you know how many serious practitioners want to get their hands on this stuff? It's like I've flown in diamonds straight from a mine, uncut."

"What's so special about it? I can get a wholesale bag of quality restaurant salt from the store for about twenty dollars."

"This salt comes from your neck of the woods. From a tribe in Ivory Coast."

"I'm from Mali," he said.

"Whatever," she shrugged. "It contains special properties to boost spell work, which makes it inedible. Mumtaz, if the magic is done right, it can affect multiple generations simultaneously. Isn't that awesome? I for one, can't wait to see my spell come to fruition."

"So, you're saying, for instance, if someone happens to be cursed…" he said.

"Uh huh," she responded.

"And, let's say, their uncles, aunts, cousins, grandparents, whatever. Let's say they're all cursed too. You're telling me that using this salt could lift it?"

"Yes."

"Really?"

"It's possible," she said.

"Mo, you gotta do this for me."

"No."

Mumtaz's smile fell. "What do you mean? Why would you say no?"

"I'm using it for something else already and I can't concentrate on two spells of that magnitude at once. Besides, your family isn't cursed."

"Sure, we are."

"Nah. You guys just suck at business."

"Hey, that's low. My family has run salt mines in Mali since forever. We were a prominent pillar in society until some jealous person in our village went to the witches at the—

"Bamako Markets and blah, blah, blah, heard it all before, my love. Let's face it. You're a fun guy sometimes, but your curse story is so boring."

His lips squeezed together in a tight line, and he ran his fingers through the dark black curls in his hair. "You really think I'm a bad businessman?"

"Honey, is water wet?" She unlatched her seatbelt and moved closer to him. "Come here," she said.

"Nah. I wouldn't want to bore you," he said, pulling away.

Mo's lips parted into a smile, then she snickered. "Don't be like that, baby. I don't think you're boring. But blaming your troubles on witchcraft is a little out there."

"How so? You're a witch."

"Yes, I am. But listen. If a real witch had a problem with you and your family, whoo boy! You'd have a lot more to worry about than that little fading line on your hand. And I wouldn't dare let anyone harm the father of my child." Mo looked into Mumtaz's eyes with a wickedly sultry look and waited for the news to register.

Mumtaz's mouth fell open and he breathed faster than the air could fill his lungs. "Me? I'm a father?"

"Don't get excited. It's very early and there's a lot you need to do to get your shit together. That's the only way that I'll agree to keep this baby, Taz. Do you understand?"

"Oh, hell no. If it's mine, you're moving in with me and we're keeping it. We're M&M's, baby. We've got to stick together."

Mo laughed, throwing her head back far enough for him to see the dark hole at the back of her throat. "That's so corny, but noble of you. I'm afraid if anyone is doing the moving, it's you. No offense to your mama and all, but I need to have my own space. But like I said, if you don't get it together, Mumtaz, this baby is going bye-bye." Mumtaz brushed the tangled wet curls away from her cheek and touched her face. Her cold skin shuddered under his hand.

"You don't have to say anything else. I know that I'm a hustler who can't seem to get it together, Mo, but I would never shirk my responsibilities."

She wrinkled her nose. "I don't want to be a 'responsibility.' That's why people end up hating each other."

"I could never hate you, Mo. You mean the world to me."

"Time will tell," she smirked.

"What are you working on, anyway?" Mumtaz asked. She'd alluded to her schemes in the past; something about getting even, but she hadn't elaborated. He couldn't decide if he should believe half of what she claimed or none of it. His father had told him long ago that magic was real. And evil. From what he could see, that was true; the only type of magic anyone ever did was the kind that made people miserable or dead. Or both.

"I'm trying to right some wrongs," she said, writing her name in the condensation on the window.

"What kinds of wrongs?"

"To be honest, it's a lot like yours. My family, my mother's family, were vilified and tortured by other folks in the community. There was a feud that ended in the wrongful death of my family members."

"And you want revenge?"

"That's right. It's owed to us."

"I don't know, people seeking vengeance rarely get what they're looking for. A lot of times, it comes back to haunt them."

"I can handle myself. It's the people I'm after who need to watch out. I plan to go for the jugular, Taz. I want to see people bleed. I want them to suffer."

"That sounds sinister as hell, Mo." A nervous chuckle escaped his lips as he buckled his seatbelt. Something about the way she smiled and gazed into the distance made him feel uneasy. He had an odd obsession for her, but sometimes, she frightened him. She seemed capable of inflicting harm on others without remorse.

"Make sure you don't get too stressed out. Not only are you responsible for your own health, but you're also taking care of the future lil Taz."

"We are not calling this kid 'lil Taz.' He'll have a respectable name if he has one at all."

"Mumtaz *is* respectable. It means 'Excellent.'"

Mo shook her head.

"What?"

"Nothing," she said, sliding back to her seat. It's a nice name."

"That's right. As I was saying, lil Taz needs your attention."

"Lil Taz won't need anything if his father doesn't get it together. I'll give you a month to start bringing in some serious cash flow and get your own place, Taz. I'm not having this baby if its father can't move out of his mother's house."

"Won't you be too far along for that kind of thing?" he asked.

"Do you think the operating table is the only way to end an unwanted pregnancy?"

Fear struck his heart. "I hear you, Mo, and I swear to you." He raised his right index finger in the air. "I will get my life in order or die trying."

Lighting crashed and his words trailed off as he caught a glimpse of the shortened line on his hand. He pressed the dome light and looked closer. "Damn."

Chapter Eight

"WHOSE NAME ARE you writing on your Hoodoo hit list this time?"
Mumtaz asked, groggy. The pitter-patter of rain outside Monet's apartment made it even more difficult to wake up.

He checked his watch and wondered why he couldn't make it to bedtime without dozing off lately. Even his sleep schedule was cursed. He'd drifted off then woke up, catching the tail-end of what she said. "Who is Victor Reneau... and who are Roxanna and Helena?"

"Enemies," Mo said, "and this ain't Hoodoo." She sat naked on the living room floor, bent over a pentacle drawn with the wax of a white pillar candle. She'd been mumbling her juju spells while he tried to take a nap. As horrific as it was to catch glimpses of her naked body covered with strange symbols painted in dove's blood, the ache in his groin wouldn't allow him to pretend he wasn't excited. At the same time, the smell made him gag a little when the breeze from the open window picked it up. Monet was a siren; she was his test from Allah, that he was failing miserably.

Mumtaz peeked at her through half-opened lids. "You should open the window. It smells like a butcher stop in here," he said, appreciating her curvaceous form as he drifted into a surreal slumber laced in erotic imagery. As his body tossed and turned on the sofa, he wondered what it is that normal couples do to pass the time.

It was impossible to lie to himself. His inner monologue told him that normal girlfriends didn't writhe and wriggle on a pentacle in the middle of the living room floor in the nude, or chant in altered voices, switching from what sounded like a child's high-pitched squeal to a strange, devilishly deep man's voice, rivaling Barry White. That shit wasn't normal.

Did men even sound like that? The weird ululations and alternating vibrato tapped into his dreams, disrupting his desire for a happy slumber, twisting his thoughts upside down, spiraling into nightmares. He sat up and snapped at her.

"What's wrong with you? How come you can't just let these people live their lives, Mo? Going to these lengths to live out some vindictive fantasy, it's just... I don't know. It's kind of sick."

"Taz, how many times have I warned you about sleeping while I work spells? Sometimes, it's a little distasteful, but I wouldn't call it sick. It's no different than working with an ailing patient in the hospital. You might need to get into a little blood and guts before you solve the problem," she said, shaking the entrails of a pigeon in his direction.

"Something is so wrong with you," he said.

"Nothing is wrong with me, Taz. Except I've got a narrow-minded, pseudo-religious boyfriend with no practical ambitions." She shot him an amused glance and tossed the handful of bones to the floor. "Interesting," she said, smiling.

He let her jabs at him slide. Mumtaz shuddered. The bones reminded him of Luqman and his pair of lucky dice. Always sevens. "What are you so happy about?"

"It looks like my plan is falling into place." She turned and whispered something into thin air, as though someone were standing there behind an invisible curtain. "Bring me something that belongs to him, something he wears. Leave it on the table," she whispered to no one he could see.

"This makes me uncomfortable, Monet. Therapy is a viable solution for whatever you're going through," Mumtaz said.

She responded by flipping him her middle finger.

"I think you need to come back from whatever dark place you're in and get out of this mess before you take it too far. You're not hurting anyone but yourself," he said.

"The pain I inflict on myself will be a thousand times worse for them," she said. Mo nodded at whatever unseen entity sat beside her and cut the palm of her hand, squeezing drops of blood onto the names scrawled on the floor. Her hand swiped the first name on the list, smearing blood across it. Victor.

Mumtaz wondered who the poor bastard was. What had he done to make a woman want him to suffer so badly that she resorted to witchcraft to inflict misery upon him?

Mo spat on the name and washed it away with a boar-bristle brush and a paste made of vinegar and baking soda. Mumtaz looked on as the mixture bubbled, bloody and fizzy until the name was gone. Everything about this woman was wrong. But his child was growing inside her. Even if he wanted to, he wasn't going anywhere now.

Mo sighed and swiped the bones off the floor, dropping them into the pouch she wore around her neck. Every time he looked, she was sporting a new type of pouch. Or was this an old one? His eyes lingered, suddenly interested in the way it dangled between her heavy breasts.

She finished her ritual, and he couldn't be more grateful. He sat still a bit longer, feeling wide awake and anxious. As was his new habit, he raised his hand to the light and studied the faded line on his palm. Creases appeared in his forehead as he tried to remember how long it had been before. "It's shorter, Mo." Mumtaz glanced at her back.

"Okay," she said, not paying attention. The other names and the pentacle became blurred streaks of reddish-pink bubbles as she moved the brush in tight, circular motions. "What are we talking about?"

"What aren't you telling me? Mo!" He waited for her to toss down her brush and look at him. "It's getting shorter."

Monet smiled, then crawled on her hands and knees until she reached his bent leg and folded her arms across his thigh, resting her chin in one hand. "Show it to me," she said. "Show me your precious hand."

Mumtaz held it up and stretched the palm wide enough for her to see what he saw. A smooth, tan-colored patch of skin, minus the palm line, except a quarter of an inch. That's all that was left of it. He held the other one up for comparison. "See? They don't match anymore. It's the curse, isn't it?"

Monet straightened up and gazed long and hard at both hands, rubbing one, then the other, feeling the differences. "I honestly don't think you're cursed, Taz. When I touch your palm and look into your aura, it's like looking into a murky puddle of water. There are ripples on the surface, but underneath is a mystery."

Mumtaz jerked his hands away and folded his arms into himself. "I thought you said that you had a gift?"

"I do, you stubborn idiot," she said, reaching for her dress folded over the back of the sofa. She put her head through it and jerked it down her body, irritated. "But it's not something I can flip on at a whim. You're probably just a freak of nature."

"I am no freak, unless you count the bedroom," he said, grabbing her ass. She slapped his hand away and retreated to an armchair opposite the coffee table.

He'd mentioned in the past that he wished she'd take a shower and wash off the blood before she touched the furniture. She'd replied that she wished he paid the rent and bought furniture so that his opinion would matter. At any rate, she hadn't told him anything about his hand that would make him worry. Not yet anyway.

"When you read palms, don't you have to turn it on at a whim?"

"Not really. People don't want to hear the truth; it would scare the shit out of them. Lying is easier."

"I want the truth, Mo. Tell me what you see. Don't hold back." He held out his hand and Mo turned away from him. "Look at me, Mo. Mo, please. Tell me what you see."

"I can't," she said, refusing to meet his eyes.

"That's great. I do so much for you every day, and you won't give me the courtesy of a reading? Where's your gratitude?"

"Don't start with me, Taz. I've had a long, hard day at work, hustling in that damned hospital, making money, I might add, and you want to lecture me about your little fading lifeline? What if I told you that a fading lifeline meant your life was fading? Would that satisfy your morbid fascination?"

Mumtaz shrank back from her. "Are you saying that my life is ending?"

"Taz, don't be stupid. I'm making a point. I said I didn't see anything. And as far as life goes? All our lives are fading. Some, just get to the finish line a little faster. That's how it works."

Chapter Nine

AFTER CLEANING HER MESS, Mumtaz talked Mo into his favorite pastime in the bedroom. He lay against the headboard, listening to her snore next to him, wondering when sleep would claim him too. The rain tapped at the window and ran down the surface of the glass in streams, slipping through the mesh of the screen every so often. The wind blew, picking up the scent of Mo's freshly washed skin.

The sex hadn't been pretty. He had complained that she expected him to touch her when she had an animal's blood dried into her pores, and she'd complained that when they were done, she'd have to wash all over again. From the looks of her clean, minimalistic apartment, you'd never guess she could be so nasty. He stared at the prisms of light reflecting from the sushi takeout across the street and focused on pushing the negative thoughts from his brain.

Mo's words had gotten to him. She always managed to say the wrong things and leave his mind in a fucked-up state. He had a child on the way. Sort of. It was still a fetus at the moment, but if he didn't start making some steady cash, Mo would get an abortion. *She wouldn't really do that, would she? It's gonna be our baby.*

She might. In that case, the sooner he arranged a meeting with Lebe, the better. He needed to fill his warehouse with whatever freaky delicacies he could get his hands on, and he was sure that guy had something that would work. Hustling for chefs was a lot more soul-sucking than he had imagined. But the money was good if you could provide.

The chefs in Rosewood Hollow would pay an arm and a leg to one-up each other. Mumtaz wondered why they would take their hard-earned talents and use them to compete in culinary depravity rather than create something delicious from pure ingredients. He supposed that turning something unabashedly disgusting into a culinary master-piece brought its own rewards. He appreciated Aminah's respectable restaurant. She used the purest ingredients she could find and respected her patrons. If he were honest instead of polite, he might tell her that she wasn't cut out for this.

Andalusia was wholesome and clean, and the food was out of this world. The place hadn't been open for very long, but he was proud of her for making it this far. She used to cater outside the masjid on Fridays and for special events, selling plates from a makeshift counter mounted in the back of her van. Everyone loved Aminah and her food. In his heart, he knew that the protestors outside her restaurant would love it too, if they didn't have chips on their shoulders about halal meat.

He was proud of her for having the courage to go after what she wanted and not be crippled by the fear of failure due to his family's misfortunes. She didn't believe in the curse. Mumtaz felt sorry for her. Sooner or later, it would come for her too.

It had come for all of them. How many cousins had they lost in the last twenty years? How many had tried to migrate north to Spain, only to drown near the Canary Islands?

Those who escaped into refugee camps had it easier, but not by much. Mumtaz remembered spending six months of his youth in the camps before a group of smiling white faces herded him, his sister and mother, two aunts, and four cousins aboard a plane headed to Virginia.

His youngest aunt, heartbroken to leave her new husband's dead body and beloved country, stared out the window, inconsolable. She refused to eat their food or drink the water sitting before her. Mumtaz couldn't understand why. Everything looked so foreign and exciting. *Different.* He asked her if he could have some of her mashed potatoes with the pat of butter melted at its center, and she gave him the whole tray.

The discovery of her cold, dead body was no surprise. It served as confirmation that the witch's reach stretched across oceans and time. The survivors were checked for hidden cyanide tablets one by one in the bathroom from head to toe by officials. They didn't appreciate spending American tax dollars on ungrateful suicidal refugees. Mumtaz wondered what scumbags meant but decided not to ask the young woman who tore at his thobe and checked his orifices while his mother watched, helpless to preserve his dignity or her own.

That was a long time ago. Mumtaz nuzzled into Monet's neck and scooped the lower portion of her belly into the palm of his hand. She squirmed against it, but quickly settled down again, snoring softly like before. A deep sigh left his lips as he thought about all he needed to do to prepare for his new family.

She'd given him so little time to turn his luck around, but he felt optimistic. He would step up and provide for her; earn her respect. Mumtaz released her and turned to face the wall. He told himself to relax, that he was down, but not out as he drifted off to sleep. His break was coming.

AT THREE IN THE MORNING, Mumtaz grimaced and sniffed the air. The stench of rotten eggs filled his nostrils and roused him from the crazy dream he'd been having. The paper mill, five minutes away by car, stank every day between three in the morning to six. Tonight, it downright reeked.

Mo slept next to him, her body as still as the night. Judging by the dry windows, the rain had stopped some time ago. Someone had turned off the takeout sign at the sushi place, but a sickly green aura hovered around it. It looked like the air smelled. Rotten.

Mumtaz sat up in the dark, gagging. Some time during the night, Mo had shut the window, but it did nothing to block the stench from entering the bedroom. He reached up and flicked a switch on the panel next to the bed. The metal blades of the industrial-style ceiling fan squeaked and came to life above them.

Cars passed by the window, illuminating the dark bedroom for a brief moment. Long shadows spread across the walls and Mumtaz watched them dance as traffic moved past the building. Branches from a tree. A light post. A hand holding a beating heart.

"What the hell?" Mumtaz shot up in bed and threw back the covers. Traffic died down again and the shadows receded. He pushed off the mattress and walked to the window.

The tree, three stories down, fluttered in the early spring breeze. The smell was stronger on this side of the bed. Mo talked in her sleep behind him.

"Kill her, and her father too..." she droned on. Mumtaz shook his head. The woman had murder on the mind.

He turned his attention back to the front of the apartment complex and scanned the sidewalk and parking lot. No one was around. Not that he'd really expected to see a person loitering with a heart in their hand. That would be insane. And scary as shit.

"A little bit of salt is enough to spread catastrophe. Don't consume it, or it will consume you," she said, turning over. A shiver passed through her body in a quick, violent wave. He covered her exposed shoulder with the duvet, then returned to the window. She kept mumbling about salt, saying something about it being spoiled. He rolled his eyes at that. *Salt doesn't spoil. It preserves.*

"Mo, babe. You're talking in your sleep," Mumtaz said over his shoulder. What was so special about that salt? It crossed his mind that a delivery truck was scheduled to drop off her order at his warehouse in the morning. He hoped it didn't take up too much space.

Of course, if it did, it was no biggie. It wasn't like he had any merchandise competing for space. Not yet. But he might, if he could convince Lebe to part with anything he found of value in the warehouse. His optimism kicked into overdrive. He'd find something. He always did.

Movement in the far-left corner of the window caught his attention. A bright red piece of fabric, flapping behind a tree. He leaned in, squinting his eyes. On second glance, he determined it was the hem of a long dress. The long, bony fingers of a woman's hand crept around the trunk. Something oval throbbed in her hand. In the dark, the complexion of the hand looked off. Green, like the sushi restaurant sign.

A deep moan escaped Mo's lips and he turned his attention back to the bed. Her shoulders continued shuddering, the movement becoming exaggerated. He turned back to the window scouring every inch of the sidewalk. Where had she gone?

He could have sworn on his father's grave that there had been a woman outside in a red dress; the same red dress worn by the woman in the cemetery a few days ago. *What was she doing here?*

Tiny veins of ice formed on the window in front of him. He touched a finger to the tiny snowflakes on the glass and sprang back from it. He stared at the window in bewilderment. It felt hot. Mumtaz looked outside again. There was no sign of the woman. He placed his fingertip on the snowflake again and it melted. It was cold like it should have been.

He chuckled to himself. *I'm losing my mind.* His erratic sleep had him believing that a woman in a nice red dress had actually been outside with a beating heart in her hand at three o'clock in the morning.

His shoulders quaked. *It's too cold.* He walked into the living room to check the thermostat. Mo's apartment building was built less than a year ago, but things went awry from time to time. Tapping sounds in the walls, dogs barking although no one had pets. Dead scorpions in the cabinets.

"This damn thing. It turns cold when the weather is cold, hot when the weather is hot. I don't understand it," he said, banging the console with his hand. A cold draft forced its way out of the vents, crackling as it collided with the warm air from his breath. He'd have to call maintenance and leave a message on their machine.

"Mumtaz, it's cold," he heard Mo say from the bedroom.

"I'm sorry about this, babe. It looks like the thermostat isn't working. Draw the blanket around yourself to keep comfortable. Mo?"

He peeked into the bedroom, glancing at the back of her head. She looked so vulnerable laying there like that. Mo could be a good woman if she'd only let him guide her. He was by no means a spiritual role model, but he knew enough to stay away from the things she dabbled in. If she were going to raise his child, he wanted it to have the purest upbringing, not one filled with the desire to mete out punishments on people.

"I don't mean to nag you about your witchy stuff, Mo. I know you have this vendetta or whatever planned, but I don't think it's healthy for you to worry about stuff like that. And seriously? The bloodletting and pigeon sacrifices can't be sanitary. I think we need to talk about our expectations for the future. Mo?"

Mumtaz walked to the bed and touched her shoulder, urging her to face him. Her body felt stiff and solid, as if she were frozen, then it jerked and convulsed under his hand. Ice from the half-frozen comforter clung to his skin.

"The hell? Mo, hold still, what are you doing? Are you alright? Are you having a seizure?"

He was of two minds about what to do. Should he move her or wait until it passed? He let her go and she flinched then pulled away from him. She slipped from his grasp and rocked off the bed. Her feet carried her towards the window where she smashed her head into the glass.

"Stop... stop it, what are you doing?" Mumtaz winced as her head cracked against the pane. He rushed to her aid and a hard backhand sent him crashing to the floor. The sound of splitting glass brought him out of his daze, and he stared in horror. Monet's head had punched a ring-shaped hole into the window.

"For the sake of Allah, Mo, stop!"

Monet came to a dead stop against the glass. The whirring sound of air whooshing from the vents settled into the background. Instead, he listened to her breathing and watched her ribcage flare and contract. The stillness in the bedroom felt stifling.

Bloody rain trickled down through the cracks in the window as she withdrew from it. She sat down on the floor with her back facing him and stretched her neck, touching the left ear to her shoulder, then repeating the movement on the other side. Sharp cracks from her neck bones made him flinch.

"Turn around, let me see your face." She didn't respond, leaving him hanging in the eerie silence, but he'd take that over watching her crack the glass with her skull. Mumtaz scooted towards her and wrapped his arms around her waist. "Damn, girl. You probably need stitches. What happened baby? Why did you do this to yourself?" He used his strength to overpower her stiff form and turned her towards him.

Mumtaz didn't see the fist connecting with his chin, but he felt the effects when his head jerked backward. His body followed, slamming into the floor. Monet pounced and straddled his midsection, forcing him to sink further down into the plush carpet.

Besides the inhuman amount of strength she possessed, her horrific gray face, black lips, and blood-red eyes freaked him out. He protected his head from the onslaught of her nails, but paid for it when she sliced his forearm to shreds. "Monet, stop!"

Monet sat up straight and opened her mouth. A powdery-white substance spilled from her lips onto Mumtaz's face, stinging his eyes and burning the membranes inside his nostrils. Salt.

Her fist bashed into his lips, splitting them as the pulverized flesh snagged on the corners of his teeth. Mumtaz thrashed under her in an unsuccessful attempt to free himself. He tasted bloody brine when he swallowed. His stomach clenched as he fought off the desire to vomit.

Her hand shot out and clasped his throat, crushing his windpipe. The built-up pressure made his head throb as he fought against her grip, throwing ineffective chops at her shoulders until he resorted to clawing at her wrists and hands. A punch might have worked, but a corner of his mind remembered the life growing inside her. His airway remained blocked, and Mumtaz panicked. Darkness crowded the edges of his vision as Monet leaned closer to his mouth.

Salt poured from her like grain from a silo harvester into his open mouth. She let go of his throat and he swallowed all of it, unable to close his mouth against the onslaught, unable to do anything but consume it. Raw salt crystals formed around his lips, and he looked down at his abdomen, swollen with his profane meal.

Mumtaz's eyes widened at the size of his distended belly. Somewhere, deep inside it throbbed and kicked against the organs and inner walls of his torso. Monet backed away from him and wiped the salt crystals off her lips. Her face appeared normal again, sweet, innocent, wiped clean of its former possession.

"What have you done to me?" His cries filled the room as something trapped inside the swell of his gut demanded its freedom. "Mo, please help me." He reached for her, and she backed away from him, afraid of her body reclaiming the infection.

His hand drew back, and he clutched his middle. The pain was unlike anything he'd ever imagined. It came in waves, starting out like a shudder, ending in seismic rings of pain around his back and lower torso, serious enough to make him consider praying. A wave of nausea overcame him, and he became sick with a frothy mix of salt and blood that burned his busted lips on its way down his chin.

A final spasm rocked him to the core, shaking his body, contracting for long beats with short bursts of release between the waves. He felt the need to bare down and push the mass out of him. Mumtaz gritted his teeth and panted until his body signaled that the time had come.

Mumtaz pushed his buttocks into the floor and looked into Monet's horrified eyes. His belly hardened and he bore down and pushed. The mass of salt tore its way out of him, ripping apart the muscled walls of his abdomen, tearing through the skin.

He screamed as a head emerged, jagged, and crystallized. The salt-crusted infant opened its mouth, searching for sustenance with its tongue. It looked like a miniature version of him.

~

"Mo!" Mumtaz called for her, clutching his belly. He opened his eyes to complete darkness and frowned. *Am I dead?* His heart pounded in his chest, but he was otherwise pain free.

The flash of lightning on the bedside table added to the confusion until he realized it was his cellphone.

"Hello?" he asked. The other end of the phone crackled. His hands still shook from the nightmare he'd had. He checked his stomach, feeling for abnormalities. A nightmare. He'd have to thank Mo for freaking him out all day with her stupid rituals.

"I think we have a bad connection. Call back," Mumtaz said.

"Mumtaz?" a broken voice said.

"Abdullah? Is that you?" He checked his watch. It was three in the morning. "As Salaamu Alaikum, cousin. Where are you? The connection is awful, man." He glanced at Monet. She was sleeping with her back to him. He shuddered. She had looked exactly like that in his nightmare.

He swung his feet over the edge of the bed then got up and walked to the living room. The room smelled like sulfur, thanks to the paper plant. "What time is it over there?"

"Can't send... shipment... the curse... Sorry... it's no good."

"Abdullah, I can't understand you. What do you mean? What about the curse? Abdullah, repeat what you said." The call dropped and Mumtaz sat down on the sofa, waiting for his cousin to call him back. The bloody handkerchief with the initials V.R. sitting on the coffee table made him forget all about the phone call. Whoever Victor Reneau was, may he rest in peace.

Chapter Ten

"It's pretty bad when your girl gets a shipment to your warehouse, but you don't," Jasim said.

"Don't you start with me, Jasim. I had a voicemail on my phone this morning. That freak, Lebe, agreed to meet with us this morning. We'll grab what we can at our meeting and then you can get off my back," Mumtaz said. Between Jasim and Mo, he was going to need every ounce of sanity he could muster to keep from cracking.

"Why are you so touchy today? And what do you mean, 'our meeting?'"

"Oh, I don't know. Maybe it was the nightmare I had last night, or it could be that I'm annoyed with all the phone calls I keep getting from a particular person." Jasim had called Mumtaz a million times to make sure the shipment from Abdullah had reached the port in Norfolk. He didn't have the heart to tell him that his cousin had bailed on him. Not with Lucky Luke looming over them.

"Hey, I've got shows to play and mouths to feed, Taz. I need to protect my fingers. So, what's in the shipping container, anyway?"

"She says it's salt."

"Why salt?"

"I don't know, man. Voodoo women need salt."

"This much? And I thought it was Hoodoo?"

"Whatever." The truck backed into the loading bay as Mumtaz and Jasim looked on. "Mo says this salt is lucrative. Apparently, she's got buyers coming from as far away as French Polynesia to get some."

"Sounds good to me," Jasim said.

"No kidding. Alright, let's get out of the way so they can unload it."

Mumtaz and Jasim watched a handful of hired men open the truck's trailer and start unpacking. An hour later, a stack of boxes sat in the middle of the modest four hundred twenty square meter warehouse.

"Yo, this is the most merchandise I've had in here at one time," Mumtaz said. He eyed the boxes with envy. He wished he had inventory that flew off the shelves. The few times he'd gotten something strange for the chefs, they'd been on the back of a refrigerated truck that drove straight to the restaurants.

"I'm gonna get something from Lebe that these chefs can't resist. It's my time to shine, Jas."

"Now you're talking. Let's go meet this cat," Jasim said.

"THANK Allah we're meeting this dude during the day. He sounds weird," Jasim said. Mumtaz glanced at the disappearing landscape in the rearview mirror and wished civilization farewell. *Feels like I'm driving us to the gates of Hell.*

At a quarter to ten, he drove past the gates of the Rosewood Hollow Cemetery on his way to White Crow Shipping and laughed. "It occurs to me that I'm less afraid of the cemetery than of going to this warehouse. Had I not been desperate, I never would have agreed to come out to this place again, day or night."

"Don't worry, man, I've got your back."

Mumtaz pulled into the parking lot and grimaced. The mist was waiting for him when he arrived. Of course, it was. A person's shadow crept against the warehouse wall, but they couldn't find its owner. "What the hell?" Mumtaz asked. Lured to this God-forsaken location of his own volition this time, Mumtaz figured the devil must be having a laugh at his expense. He half-expected a ghost to saunter by and give him the finger.

His car was the sole vehicle in the lot. The overcast sky grew dark, and a lone bulb flickered on in the far-right corner of the lot. "For a warehouse, this place sure is dead. When does it jump?"

"Most likely, it's during the graveyard shift," Jasim said. Mumtaz laughed at the joke, but the sound of his voice made him nervous. *Seriously though, how do truckers pass through the weighing stations with all that strange shit? And when do they unload them?*

He parked at the front door entrance and cut the engine. His hand reached for the door, then hesitated. He needed a moment to collect himself before meeting with this guy. "How does Mo not get the creeps around Lebe? Witch or no witch, you'd think she'd catch strange vibes from this dude and stay the hell away."

"What was that?" Jasim asked, craning his neck to look out the sunroof.

"It sounded like something brushed across the top of the car."

"Maybe it was a low-hanging tree branch, like the ones at my mother's house in the driveway. She's gonna kill me because I keep forgetting to trim them."

"There's no trees on this side of the lot, and the car ain't moving," Jasim said.

"Then, what was it?" Mumtaz looked up but didn't see anything. He cracked the sunroof open, locked the latch, and waited. Nothing.

He heard the noise again, this time in three quick intervals, too fast to decipher what was happening. "Were those birds?"

"Whatever it was, it moved fast," Jasim said. Puzzled, they leaned close to the window and peered upward, but the angle was no good. Again, three quick swoops, then a slower, clumsy swipe and a tumble. Some big and heavy thing crashed into the sunroof, leaving a deep crack.

"Shit!" Mumtaz jumped. The sound reminded him of thin ice cracking on the surface of a pond. The thing tore itself from the latch and flung itself down the windshield and onto the hood of the car. It landed on the sidewalk with a thick, meaty smack. Mumtaz and Jasim sat there, transfixed by fear and curiosity.

"You should check it out," Jasim said.

"I ain't checking shit." Mumtaz's hands dug into the steering wheel while the blood froze in his veins. He didn't dare get out; watching the heaving lump from the safety of his vehicle was sufficient. Dark energy pulsed in the dead air as the creature writhed on the ground. Mumtaz swallowed three or four times to get the saliva running in the desert of his mouth and leaned in for a closer look.

He nearly shit himself when a knock clattered the passenger window. Mumtaz peered at a shape outside the car. His eyes adjusted, separating the black-skinned man from the night. Lebe.

"Hey, you're early," Lebe said. He paused for a beat and smiled with his freakishly straight white teeth. Mumtaz squirmed in his seat. Was it worth his sanity to put up with this bullshit, or should he start the car and burn rubber? "What's wrong, Mister Busri? Cat got your tongue?"

"Man, there's something out there," Mumtaz said.

Lebe looked around. "Where? I don't see nothing."

"Over there," Mumtaz pointed. He frowned. "It was there a minute ago."

Lebe walked toward the front of the vehicle and looked around. "I don't see a thing. I think your mind is playing tricks on you, my friend."

"And Jasim's mind too?" Mumtaz asked.

"It is my experience that friends can be collectively crazy," Lebe said.

"What did he say?" Jasim asked, releasing his seatbelt.

Mumtaz got out and walked to the front of the car. The figure was gone. He shook his head. "This place freaks me out... How can you work here? Doesn't it fuck with your mind?"

Lebe clapped a hand on Mumtaz's shoulder. "There's only one thing that messes with my mind. Women. Come on inside. We can discuss business."

～

"Taz, your girl is in league with the devil," Jasim whispered into Mumtaz's ear.

Mumtaz elbowed Jasim in the ribs and raised an eyebrow in warning. He didn't want Lebe to hear him, even though the tall, slender man was on the phone with his back turned as they examined the strange merchandise. He had given them a photocopy of a hand-drawn map with the permitted viewing areas outlined in white, and danger zones in red.

"You know, I don't remember this warehouse being here," Jasim said. I could have sworn this was a gas station or something."

Mumtaz shook his head. "The gas station is further down the road, near the cemetery. Mo says this place has been here for ages."

"Maybe we didn't notice because the place is creepy as hell," Jasim said, stopping in the middle of a row. "Why would anybody need a bag of rooster beaks?"

"Soup base?"

"With beaks?"

"Man, how am I supposed to know? According to this map, exotic meats are over here in this section," Jasim said, pointing. They walked to the end of the aisle and turned the corner.

The aisle opened up into a well-lit supermarket display of packaged, bloodied things that would make the wildest hog think twice. "What the hell kind of place have you brought me to, Taz? The place should be called, 'Satan's Food Mart.' Where are the Baphomet cookies with Iblis sprinkles?"

"You can wait at the front if you want," Mumtaz said.

"With Papa Legba? No thanks."

"For a guy who professes not to know a lot about the occult, you know a lot about the occult," Mumtaz said, scanning the refrigerated section. There were packages of bushmeat and chevaline ready to go. "This could work," Mumtaz said, getting his phone out.

"Do you really think your chefs would go for this?" Jasim asked, poking at the packages with a bottle of hot sauce.

"I'm counting on it," Mumtaz said, snapping pictures. "They love this disgusting crap."

"Have you ever tried any of it?"

Mumtaz's phone hand dropped to his side. "How long have you known me?"

"Forever," Jasim said.

"Then why would you ask me that?"

"Well, you're not opposed to selling it for other people to eat. How do I know your sense of decency hasn't been compromised? I mean, look at where we're standing, Taz."

"My sense of decency may be altered, but I'm still your boy."

"And you want to feed people something that came out of this place? I mean, we can pretty much guess that nothing's halal—hell, we know it ain't kosher either. But, Taz, this place is fucked up."

Mumtaz sighed. "Maybe you're right. Maybe my sense of decency has altered. But have you forgotten about Luqman? If I don't sell something, he's gonna take my head."

"And my fingers, no thanks to you," Jasim said.

"Then we agree? I have to sell something out of this place, or you'll lose your livelihood." Mumtaz reached into the refrigerator and pulled out a long grayish-looking leg of an animal Jasim didn't recognize and hoisted it over his shoulder. "I hope these fit in my car."

Jasim stared at his fingers, opening, and closing them while he thought. "I don't want you doing this for me, Taz. This is crazy. Put that back and take me home."

"Stop playing, Jasim. Buck up and grab a couple of these elephant legs."

"I mean it. I'd rather lose my fingers than have you selling stuff like this. Put it back. I don't want to be associated with any of this. I'll make some calls and see what I can do about the money."

Mumtaz looked his friend in the eyes. One way or another, he felt like the biggest scumbag on earth. "Fine. I'll put it back." He unshouldered his burden, tossing it back into the refrigerator bed. "I want you to remember this moment if anything goes wrong from here."

"You got it. Let's get out of here." Jasim spun on his heels and high-tailed it to the front of the warehouse. Mumtaz hung back. Jasim was at his limit, but time was of the essence. He had hoped his friend would be on board with this. Clearly, he'd have to do this on his own when he wasn't around.

"Is there a problem with the merchandise?" Lebe stepped out of the shadows.

"Damn, man, you're like a cat. And no, it's my friend's moral sensibilities that are holding me back."

"That's a pity. You could fetch a handsome price for a truckload of bushmeat."

"I know. Listen. I'm gonna drop him off then come back here, okay?"

"Sorry, it's now or never."

"How come?"

"I have a life, you know."

Mumtaz shuddered, wondering what this man could possibly do in his spare time that wasn't a crime against nature.

"I can't take it now; he'd freak out on me."

"Sounds like you've got a problem with your buddy. Maybe you should put him in his place and take the merchandise anyway."

"Maybe you should stay out of it," Mumtaz said.

"Just trying to help. Of course, you could borrow a little of your girlfriend's order."

"To sell on my own?"

"Sure. She probably hasn't sold all of it yet."

"She hasn't sold any of it," Mumtaz said, stroking his chin. After all the big talk about being better at his business than he was, Mo hadn't opened a single bag of what he suspected was plain old table salt.

"There you go. You'd be doing her a favor. And what restaurant doesn't need salt? A woman looks up to a man who takes charge and relieves her of her burdens."

"It's a good point," Mumtaz said.

"It's a great point," Lebe said, flashing his white teeth.

Chapter Eleven

"THERE'S MORE of it than I expected. Maybe you can get some retailers to take it off your hands." Jasim's eyes traveled from the floor to the ceiling, taking in the stacked packages of unboxed salt. He seemed to brighten up when Mumtaz told him that Lebe suggested they sell Mo's salt instead of the sketchy stuff from what he coined the 'deep web freezer.'

"I don't have the connections to move this kind of product right now, so we'll see how profitable this turns out to be."

"How are you an importer of goods without connections?"

Mumtaz shrugged. "I'm working on it. I don't know anybody who'll want this much salt in a hurry. I might be able to peddle some to the local restaurants and work out a deal over time, but I need money now."

"Ask Aminah. She might want to get in on it."

"I can't keep dealing with her."

"Why not? You know she won't say no."

"That's precisely why I don't want to take more money from her. No matter how much I screw up, I end up taking too much away from her in the end. That's not right."

"Well, you'd better take it from somebody, or Luke's gonna deal with both of us." They both stared in silence at the salt, trying to figure out the next move.

"Maybe you can learn to play the bass with your thumbs and pinkies."

"Not cool, Taz."

"Alright, alright. Let me make some phone calls."

∼

L ATER THAT DAY, Mumtaz climbed out of his car and strolled up the walk to Mo's apartment building carrying a bouquet of cheap wildflowers and a bottle of sparkling grape juice. It was funny how Mo did all the nasty stuff one could imagine, but she didn't drink alcohol.

He felt tired, but in a good way. He hadn't put in an honest day's work in a while, and it made all the difference in his mood.

Today, he had sat in his office chair in a corner of the warehouse and actually called potential buyers. After a lot of slick words and coy promises, he had a few of his usuals who'd been less than enthused with his last offerings come through. First up, Chef Anna Dupree.

They agreed to get the ball rolling first thing in the morning. Chef Anna got on her social media accounts and boasted that her special contact was bringing something magical for her. Her words, not his.

After that, his phone rang off and on throughout the day. All he had to do was take down the appointments. Things were back on track. Somewhat.

If he couldn't come up with the money in time, he hoped Jasim would ask around for it. Mumtaz knew that "ask around" meant asking his new mother-in-law to loan him the money behind his wife's back.

If Nyah found out, it was lights out for both of them anyway. She didn't like Jasim or anyone else messing with her mother's small nest egg. He didn't blame her. If his mother had retirement money, he wouldn't want anyone messing with his future inheritance either.

The elevator doors opened, and he stepped out. His nose was met with a fragrance he had grown to loathe. Black tulips. The flowers were a hideous result of crossbreeding that Mo's ex-boyfriend, a nobody cop on the police force, grew in his backyard. He hoped the guy had left already.

He felt around in the large potted plant separating the doorway of her apartment and the one next door for the extra key, but it wasn't there. For some reason, he wanted the guy to see him with the key and think he lived there too, although a keen eye would tell him that none of his belongings were there. She allowed a toothbrush and a few pairs of his boxers, but otherwise, he wasn't supposed to leave his stuff at her place.

His hand slipped further into the pot, disturbing the top layer of soil. *Where was the damn key?* He gave up and set the flowers and bottle on the floor to dust off his hands. As he slapped them together, the door opened. Mumtaz quickly bent over to pick them up.

"Aren't you sweet? Girls love gifts. I'd say you're a keeper."

Mumtaz's blood ran cold. It was the woman from his nightmare, the one carrying the bloody heart. The red dress, which she still wore, looked dangerously vibrant next to her skin, which had a slight greenish tint. If he didn't know better, he'd think she died a few hours ago. Instinct kicked in, and Mumtaz backed away from her.

"What's wrong, Mumtaz? I'm not gonna hurt you," she said, stepping closer. "I only hurt people when I'm asked. You have nothing to fear. Not from me, anyway."

"That's enough." Detective Norman Hanzlik stepped outside the apartment and grabbed the woman by the elbow, steering her towards the elevator. "Let's go."

"Alright, you don't have to shove, Norman," the woman said. Her voice sounded distorted; not human, but close.

"How are you doing, Mumtaz? Oh, can you give this to Monet for me? I've told her a hundred times not to leave it in that pot. You never know what loser will use it to get into her apartment." The detective smiled, pink-faced with yellowing teeth. *Like a dirty, conniving pig.*

Norman dropped the key into Mumtaz's jacket pocket and stepped into the awaiting elevator. The doors eased together, and Norman's hand shot out, forcing them open. "By the way, I hear you knocked her up. Between you and me, the last person on earth I'd trust around a baby is an ambitious witch, especially one in the Tansy family. If I were you, I'd be planning my exit strategy."

"You're not me," Mumtaz said.

"No, my friend, I'm not. Anyway, gotta run. People are dropping dead in this city like you wouldn't believe. I have a feeling we're just getting started." Norman removed his hand and the doors shut. Mumtaz hoped he never saw the old bastard ever again.

~

"WHAT ARE THE FLOWERS FOR? What's wrong?" Mo took the wildflowers and placed them in a tall white vase with water.

"Why does something have to be wrong for me to bring flowers to my girl?"

"That's what I'd like to know," she said. "You never bring them until you've done something wrong, so let's hear it."

He passed her a glass of sparkling grape juice. "Nothing's wrong, baby. Things are getting back on track, and I think that's worthy of a celebration, don't you?"

Monet eyed him, lips pressed to the edge of the glass. She studied him in a way that made alarm bells go off in his head, bringing forth every guilty thing she didn't know about to the surface. After an excruciating pause, she sipped her drink.

"Good?"

"Hmm. What did Norman say to you?" she asked.

"Why do you think he said anything?"

"Because he doesn't like you. And he's a cop. He told me you were the type to get into hot water and that I'd better get used to being alone."

"What an asshole. He told me that I should leave you."

"Is that so?" She smiled to herself.

"Doesn't that make you upset?"

"No, he's jealous."

"Jealous?" Mumtaz didn't think he sounded jealous, but he didn't know him well. "Who was that woman with him?"

"That's no woman," Mo said. "The less you know about it, the better."

"I think I've seen her a couple of times before. She was in my dream last night."

Mo frowned. "Do you still pray before bed?"

"What do you mean?"

80

"I think it's a straightforward question."

"Nah. You don't pray either."

"No, but I do make sure nothing is able to bother me while I'm sleeping. You don't wanna play around when you sleep at my house, Taz. Be a good boy like when I first met you and say your prayers."

"Is that why you love me? Because I'm a good boy?"

"Well, it ain't because you're a successful businessman, is it?"

The smile fell from his face. "Why do you always say shit like that?"

"Honest shit?"

"Hurtful. I'm doing my best out there every day. Do you know how exhausting it is to supply my sophisticated clientele?"

"You're catering to a bunch of freaky chefs who only pull a crowd when they cook something weird."

"I'm fulfilling a niche that is very in demand."

"If it's so in demand, why do you still live with your mother?"

"You know what? I've had enough from you today, Mo. Your ex has really gotten into your head. I'll see you later."

"Bye."

Mumtaz grabbed his jacket and headed for the door. He'd show her. Not only would he make enough money to pay back Luqman, but he'd also sell every grain of salt in the damned warehouse.

"THIS IS what I've waited for? Salt?" Chef Anna could not have scrunched her face together any tighter in irritation.

"I'm sorry, Chef. I know it's not what you were expecting—"

"Why should I buy it from you?"

"Because I need a favor?"

"Pssht. We all need those." Chef Anna referred to tiny scribbles in the margins of her notebook as she stirred a batch of béchamel sauce. She had a small army of chefs stocking food items inside the kitchen pantries and freezers, in anticipation of the big opening. He recognized some of them from her other establishments and gave them curt nods.

Chef Tomás shouted orders from the butchering area from time to time at the ones who rested too long in the back of the kitchen near the mop sink. Mumtaz felt like gagging when he saw the chef's bloody apron with bits of bone and entrails on it. He wanted to run outside and let the wind carry away the smell of pie crust, raw, bloody meat, and paint.

"What'd you bring us, Taz?" Chef Tomás asked, wiping his hands on a kitchen towel.

"Salt—West African salt," he said, jazzing it up. "From Ivory Coast."

"It's an interesting color," the chef said, squeezing between Chef Anna and Mumtaz. "See this pinkish color? There are bits of red clay in it." He used a clean spoon to push around the granules. "May I?" he asked Mumtaz.

"Sure."

"Do you think it's a good idea to buy salt with such large quantities of clay, Tomás?" Chef Anna asked.

"It's perfectly safe, Anna," Chef Tomás said. "Red clay is good for the body in modest quantities. There's lots of calcium, and other minerals. It's good for digestion, also. The danger is in eating too much."

"How come?" she asked.

"It's addictive," Chef Tomás said. He darted his tongue at the spoon, picking up granules of salt.

"I don't have a problem with that," Chef Anna said. "I want everyone to become addicted to my food."

Chef Tomás whispered something in her ear and passed her the spoon. She tasted it and glanced at Tomás. He nodded. Mumtaz watched the exchange in silence, wondering what they thought of it.

Chef Tomás turned to Mumtaz. "We'll take three—"

"Six," Chef Anna said.

"Six bags?" Mumtaz asked. He couldn't believe his good fortune.

"Six pallets," Chef Tomás said.

"Come again?" He stopped typing their request into his phone and waited for clarification. "How much?"

"Six pallets," Chef Tomás repeated.

"Seven," Chef Anna said.

"I'll send a delivery truck," Mumtaz said before they changed their minds.

"And I'll write you a check," Chef Anna said. She poured the rest of the salt into her mouth. Mumtaz's face was a mixture of a smile and a cringe.

≈

"LET ME GET THIS STRAIGHT. You've got salt. Not Himalayan or Greek artisanal salt. This is…"

"West African salt." After Chef Anna wrote Mumtaz's check, he headed over to Brimstone's to see if Chef Malcolm would buy it. He could be a pain in the butt, but one mention of Anna Dupree and he'd at least sample it.

Chef Malcolm pinched the bridge of his nose. "Taz, what am I going to do with—how much did you say?"

"Seven pallets."

"Seven pallets with fifty or so bags of West African salt. White table salt?"

"It's not white. It has flecks of color in it. It's… earthy."

"But it's salt, right? Are you out of your mind? Why so much?"

"You won't have to buy anymore for a long time," Mumtaz said.

"No shit. But I don't need it, Taz. We haven't put saltshakers on the dining tables in ten years. And we don't use that much salt where I'd need to buy tons of it."

"At least humor me. Give it a taste, Chef. Maybe you'll change your mind."

Chef Malcolm sighed. "Fine. Hand it over, Taz."

"Here you go." Mumtaz pushed a small bowl of salt towards Chef Malcolm and waited for the chef to tell him to get lost.

The chef dipped his pinky in the salt like it was cocaine and dotted his tongue with it. The indifference on Chef's face turned to utter shock. Then, he licked his forefinger, dipped it into the bowl and coated his tongue with salt.

Mumtaz frowned on his behalf. "Chef, it's not sugar, it's—"

"Delicious," Chef Malcolm said, standing. "I'll take the whole thing right now."

"You will?" Mumtaz tried to find the sarcasm in the chef's statement.

"Yes. How soon can you get it here? Do I need to pay for transport? I'm willing to do whatever it takes." Chef Malcolm went back to dipping and licking salt off his fingers.

"I'll deliver the product to you for free if you accept my asking price," Mumtaz said. He felt sick watching the man eat from the bowl. "D-do you want some bottled water, Chef? That's a lot of salt you're eating."

"But it's so damn good, Taz. I can't stop eating it," Chef Malcolm said.

"Okay, I'm glad you like it," Mumtaz said, taking a swig from his bottle of water. "Let's talk about the price."

~

"DAMN. I'm late for dinner. My mom is going to nag me to no end if I don't get out of here."

"We're almost done. Did you tell Chef Malcolm that you sold six pallets to Chef Anna this morning?" Jasim asked. Since his musical career lay on the line, he'd insisted on helping Mumtaz see through the task of selling the salt.

"Didn't have to. He tasted it and went crazy."

"Why do you keep selling to her first?"

"Because she's the trendsetter. If it makes her happy to think she's the only one in town getting a certain product, or at least a lower price, so be it."

"What if he finds out you're selling it to her for such a low price?"

Mumtaz shrugged. "They're classy enough to not do that. And if they aren't, who cares?" He looked at his buzzing phone and frowned. "Oh, my God."

"What?" Jasim rolled a bag of salt onto a dolly cart.

"Chef Anna's asking for eight more pallets for tomorrow," Mumtaz said, staring at the screen. "My luck is finally turning around."

Jasim shook his head and glanced at the bags. "What the hell's in this stuff?"

Chapter Twelve

MUMTAZ WEAVED THROUGH TRAFFIC, arriving at his mother's house more late than fashionable. His mother's car and four others sat in the gravel driveway ahead of his own. *Shit. Everybody's here.*

He had hoped to sneak in a few minutes ahead of everyone to speak with her alone. It was time to inform her about Monet and the baby. Fat chance of that happening now. Not only was his sister here, but his cousins had arrived too.

"As Salaamu Alaikum." The greeting escaped Mumtaz's lips and fell on deaf ears. Assuming they were on the deck, he kicked off his shoes at the front door and wedged them onto the overstuffed shoe rack. He heard a car pull into the driveway and opened the door to see who it was.

His dark brown complexion turned ashen at the sight of Mo climbing out of a car. She slammed the door and waved the driver off, then turned towards the house.

"What the hell is this?" He knew his worlds were going to collide, but he wanted it to be on his own terms, in his own time. Conversations needed to happen first.

"Hey, babe!" Mo slinked up the driveway, tan legs peeking out from the split in his favorite dress, and anxiety washed over him. The idea of Mo meeting his mother in *that* dress brought on ill feelings. This was all wrong.

"What are you doing here, Mo?"

"I saw Jasim at the mall a few minutes ago. He mentioned you were having a big family get-together at your mother's house."

"He did?" Was Jasim tripping or something? Why would he tell her about the family coming over? Was he still upset about Luke, even though he knew the situation was under control now?

"I figured, since I'm pregnant, it's time that I meet her, don't you think?" Monet rubbed her belly and he winced.

"You should have called first. I don't know if they made enough food for an extra person," he said. The words sounded lame, but he had to think of something.

"That's alright, I'm not hungry anyway. The morning sickness has kicked in." She hiked up the bottom of her dress and climbed the porch stairs.

"If you want, you can take my car and go somewhere until I'm through," he said. "The tank's almost full. I'll call you when I'm done."

"What? Where would I go? Don't you want me to meet your mama?"

"There are plenty of things that you could do. Run some errands or go see a movie." He dug into his pocket and handed her forty dollars. "My treat."

Monet broke out into full-on laughter and gave him back the money. "I'm not going anywhere, Taz. Loosen up. Let's go visit your people." She pushed him into the house with an open hand and looked around. "This is exciting. I never got to know my mother. I feel like this is the start of a new beginning. I'm sorry that I treated you badly the other night. I was in a shitty mood when Norman left. By the way, where is everybody?"

"On the deck. Take off your shoes."

"Why do I have to remove my shoes?"

"Because that's what we do here." He pointed to the overflowing shoe rack and the pile of tiny ones next to it.

"I don't want to. I'm not wearing any socks."

"Don't worry. My mom has a little basket of slippers."

"I'll pass. It's kind of weird being barefoot at a stranger's house. It's even weirder to wear their slippers."

"Why are your feet green on the bottom?" he asked.

"I was in the park last night, preparing a spell. That's why I don't want to take off my shoes. Grass stains."

"You couldn't take a shower afterwards?"

"It's just my feet. I planned to give them a good scrubbing later," she said.

"You can wait in the car, you know." Mumtaz said it louder than he meant to and watched her face scrunch.

"Damn, Taz, that's cold."

"Please, Mo, don't talk about your magic crap here. Just play along and I'll get us out of here as soon as possible. The slippers are brand new, by the way. You can take them with you and wear them again next time." If there was a next time. His mother would probably throw him out for this.

They turned towards the sound of multiple light footfalls on the stairs. It was Aminah and her one-year-old son, Hashim.

"As Salaamu Alaikum, Mumtaz," Aminah said. "Auntie is upset because you're late. Hello." Aminah paused on the last stair and gave Monet a once-over. She tilted her head at her cousin and waited for an explanation.

"Hi," Monet said, waving.

"This is Monet," Mumtaz said. "She's a friend. Mo, this is my youngest cousin, Aminah and her son, Hashim."

"Nice to meet you," Aminah said, eyeing her cousin. "Nobody mentioned you were bringing a guest."

"It was kind of a spur of the moment thing," he said, playing with a stray curl near the back of his collar.

"Ooh, Uncle's gonna get it." The three adults turned towards the kitchen. A little girl stood in the doorway, holding a popsicle and grinning from ear to ear.

"Don't be a brat, Leylah. Be quiet," Mumtaz said to his sister's nine-year-old daughter. Leylah had a knack for eavesdropping. If she was around, you'd better not say anything you didn't want everyone else to hear.

Aminah guided her son towards the girl and gave her the little boy's hand. "Leylah, take Hashim and go outside. Now."

Leylah snapped to attention and took her cousin through the

kitchen. When the patter of soft feet hitting the floor stopped and the sliding patio door whooshed open, then closed, Aminah turned back to her cousin and Monet.

"Is this a date?"

"No..." Mumtaz said.

"Kind of," Monet answered. "I'd like to see what I may be getting into if Taz and I get more serious. It's kind of a preliminary meeting."

Aminah faced Mumtaz. "And you thought it would be good to do this now, in front of everyone with no warning? Auntie doesn't like surprises."

"Chill out, Aminah. I know it's not a good look, cousin, but let's make the most of it, okay? Can you help me out and have my back out there?"

Aminah took in a deep breath then let it out. "I guess I don't have a choice."

~

THE CHATTER from the dinner party came to an abrupt halt when Aminah opened the sliding door. No doubt, Leylah had blabbed to everyone about Monet. Mumtaz stepped onto the crowded deck after Aminah with Monet bringing up the rear. Mumtaz heard the door close behind him, cutting off his escape from this awkward situation.

"Salaam, everybody," he said, trying to sound casual.

"Hi," Monet said, waving. Mumtaz winced. Aminah joined her son at the table, placing him onto her lap while he and Monet waited.

"You're late." His sister, Hidaya, glared at him from across the table. He hated the way she sucked up to their mother. She practiced a rigid version of their religion, and acted like her lifestyle was the defacto. He hated her unyielding and judgmental attitude. At times, she could be a bitch. Hidaya sat next to his brother-in-law, Jamal, who had yet to look up from his plate. *Trained puppy.*

"Sorry about that. I got held up."

"By what?" Aminah's sister, Nafisa, glared at him from the other end. Her husband, Malik, mimicked Jamal's body language, choosing to concentrate on his salad. Aminah's other brother-in-law, Yusuf, tended the grill. His wife, Sadiya, gulped her iced tea, trying to hide her grin. It was as big as Leylah's.

When Mumtaz found the nerve, he met his mother's eyes, taking in the appalled expression on her face. "Sorry I'm late, Ma. Mo, come here. This is Monet, everyone. Monet needed a ride." He felt Mo's head jerk in his direction, but he refused to look at her.

"Why didn't you give Monet a ride then? Why did you bring her here?" Hidaya asked. His cousin, Sadiya snickered.

"I asked to meet you all," Monet said, stepping around him and pulling up a chair next to Malik. His eyes bounced from Monet to his wife and back to his plate.

Malik tried sliding his chair away from her, closer to Jamal's. "Everything smells lovely, Missus Busri," Monet said, grabbing a paper plate and plastic cutlery. Mumtaz's mother didn't speak, but her scowl told him everything he needed to know.

"Monet, I don't recall my brother mentioning you before. Do you attend our masjid?" Hidaya asked. Mumtaz sucked his teeth loud enough for his sister to hear it. She knew damn well that Monet didn't go to their masjid.

"Please, call me Mo. And no, I don't go to your masjid. I'm not Muslim," she said. Aminah waved to Yusuf, and he brought over a piping hot plate of grilled chicken.

"Have some, Mo," Aminah said, passing a bowl of salad from her end of the table.

"Thanks," Monet said, getting comfortable. "Aren't you going to eat, Taz?"

"Yes, *Taz*, you should have some too. Yusuf has been keeping the grill hot for you. It would be an insult not to eat," Nafisa said.

"Sure, I'll have some," he said, reaching for a plate.

"Are you Jewish, Mo, or perhaps a Christian?" Hidaya asked.

"No. I'm a pagan. I practice magic through my ancestors, mostly using Hoodoo, but I dabble in modern witchcraft too." The table went quiet.

"Pagan?" Hidaya asked, her fork frozen in front of her lips.

"Yes, I worship the natural world and make use of all that the ancestors provide me as gifts," she said. Mumtaz felt heat rise to his face, turning his dark skin a plum-colored hue.

"Astaghfirullah," someone hissed.

"Uh, what do you do for a living?" Aminah asked.

"I'm a nurse," Monet said. Mumtaz's anxiety eased off a little, and his tongue reached for the chicken hanging out of his mouth.

"And sometimes I read palms at Crystal Falls and sell magical supplies through my website."

"The mall? You read palms at the mall?" Sadiya asked.

"She's a nurse," Mumtaz said.

"Yes, at the mall," Monet said. "It's a part-time gig where I can use my talents and earn some extra cash. Living alone is expensive. I don't have a grown son to help me pay the bills," Monet said, laughing. "In the meantime, I'll need to get ready for when your grandchild arrives." The entire table fell into a shocked silence. For some time, the curious bees and a couple of rogue flies were the only ones providing conversation.

Mumtaz swallowed the dry lump of chicken in his mouth and chased it with water. His teeth hurt as the iced liquid passed over them and traveled down his throat. *The one time Ma allows ice water.* His brain hurt too; he couldn't tell if it was from brain freeze or this awkward situation.

"You're a pagan, palm-reading nurse? How do you know my brother?" Hidaya asked.

"Oh, we met at the—"

"Enough!" Everyone turned their attention to Mumtaz's mother. "How about we don't ask Mumtaz's guest for her entire life story and finish our food?" she asked.

"Thank you, Ma, I...." The words got stuck in Mumtaz's throat. His mother glared at him with daggers in her eyes. He turned his attention to his plate and picked at his salad. The sky rumbled. Soon, the bottom would fall out of it.

"Do you mind if I use your bathroom?" Monet asked. "I have to go a lot more lately."

"Sure," Aminah said, cutting off Hidaya. "It's past the kitchen, down at the end of the hall on the right."

Monet hopped up from the table and disappeared into the house. Mumtaz, who had switched to cold iced tea, waited for the onslaught. It never came. To his horror, the family continued eating as if nothing happened. He set the glass on the table and looked from one family member to the next.

Their stone faces revealed neither consternation nor empathy. Except for Aminah. She gave her head a gentle shake, then raised an eyebrow. Now was not the time, but Mumtaz raised his in return, then alternated back and forth. Aminah's laughter burst from her lips before she could stop it. The others pretended not to hear.

Good old Aminah. Even when he was wrong, he could count on her to relieve the pressure. As for the rest of them, they gave him no mercy. He was ten years old again, eating a plate of salad and vegetables with no meat. A dark thought sapped his inappropriate humor. Who would die this time when he tried to fix things?

⁓

"THAT WASN'T SO BAD, was it?" Monet put her twists into a messy bun and strapped on her seatbelt.

"I'll never hear the end of it. My mother's going to disown me," Mumtaz said, starting the car and pulling out of the driveway. He didn't fasten his seatbelt until he was a mile down the road. "Hidaya just couldn't keep her mouth shut, could she?" he asked.

"I'll never keep your sister and cousin's names straight. Except Aminah. She's different from the others. Very sweet. The others will get over it, Taz, we caught them off guard," Monet said.

"You think? Sweetheart, I told you to take the car and go somewhere, anywhere far from my mother's house. Why didn't you go?"

"I didn't want to be alone," she said. "I feel a little vulnerable today." Her purse vibrated on the armrest, and she took out her cellphone and stared at the display.

"Who is it?" Mumtaz asked.

"Wait a minute," Monet said, answering. "Hey, what's up? Be careful. No one saw me except the old man who cuts the grass on the golf course. I gave you what you wanted... He had it coming. If I hadn't sent her, he would have figured it out. Yes, the tulips. He's seen me with them. I don't want you to get into trouble. Okay. You too. Bye."

"What was that all about? Who had it coming?"

"Trust me, you don't want to know."

"I do want to know, Mo. It's that cop, isn't it? What's he got you involved with now?"

"Relax, Taz. Norman has been tying up loose ends since his wife's death, and I'm helping him."

"Does this have anything to do with Victor Reneau?"

Mo's mouth twitched. "Taz, will you drop it?"

"I saw something a few nights ago."

"Taz..."

"I thought it was a dream or something. There was a handkerchief on the table. Maybe I was already awake, I can't remember."

"Will you fucking forget about Victor Reneau? He's dead."

"How did he get that way?" He wished he hadn't asked, but it escaped his lips before he could stop it.

"Ask the police," she said.

"You mean, ask that crooked cop, Norman." Mumtaz gripped the steering wheel and slammed the pedal into the floor. Whatever she was doing, he hoped the cop wasn't manipulating her.

She smirked. "Yeah, I'm sure he'll fill you in on all the details."

"I hope for your sake he hasn't dragged you into something illegal," he said.

"Yeah, like selling monkey meat off the back of a truck is legal. I can handle myself," she said.

"It was a zebra, and it was refrigerated. Do you still have feelings for this guy? I mean, I'm the one you love now, right?"

"I don't want to go home yet," Mo said. "Take me somewhere fun, Taz. I need to forget about all this drama."

"Can't you give me a straight answer just once in your life?"

"Come on, Taz. Lighten up. I'll make it up to you tonight." He let out a sigh and took the ramp leading to the highway.

Chapter Thirteen

THE TWENTY-MINUTE WAIT to get into the jazz lounge at Josephine's was worth it. Mumtaz hadn't seen a show in ages, and the energy of the crowd stirred him into a frenzy.

Hearing Jasim complain about the politics and drama within the house band was a drag, but Mumtaz swelled with pride watching him perform. That was his friend on stage, improvising around the melody, and plucking relentlessly at the strings of an upright bass like he had one night to live. Mumtaz's cellphone buzzed but he chose to ignore it. This was Jasim's moment.

He studied his friend's hands as Jasim summoned each note with the pluck of his fingers. The mouth-watering scent of cinnamon from the upstairs bakery permeated the space, making it a full sensory experience. He was glad Mo suggested they go out. The atmosphere helped him forget about the fiasco at his mother's house for a little while.

Jazz was the one point of contention in Jasim's household. Music, forbidden by most Islamic scholars, drove a wedge between him and his wife. It was the one thing he appreciated about Mumtaz. He never judged Jasim's passions.

He wanted to tell his friend how cool he looked on the stage, how awesome he was for bending the instrument to his will. Mumtaz made a silent commitment to him. He'd get them out of this mess with Luqman and be a better friend in the future. If he failed, well, he didn't want to think about that.

"These are awesome seats," Monet said, clinking her long black nails on her glass. Mumtaz glanced at her and found it curious how the same outfit that brought shame to him at his mother's house was now more than appropriate in the jazz club. Candlelight spilled across her brown shoulders. Mumtaz couldn't help himself. He bent towards her and kissed her neck. The phone in his pocket rang between them.

"Taz, no," she said, leaning away from him.

"What's the problem? I'm not even doing anything."

"Just don't, okay? I feel nauseous. Let's enjoy the music."

"Fine." Mumtaz gritted his teeth and turned away from her. If she didn't want to be bothered with him, she could go back to her cop. Mumtaz should have taken her home and left her there. Pretty as she was under the dazzling lights, he didn't need a cold, second-hand woman. But then, he remembered the baby.

His pocket vibrated again. Mumtaz reached into it, unable to ignore the incessant buzzing. Monet nodded to the beat, lost in her own world.

"I'll be right back," he said, tapping her on the arm.

"Okay." She kept her eyes on the stage and reached for her mocktail.

Mumtaz shook his head and walked out of the lounge. She used to be so hot for him all the time. Back when his bank account was full. Now, she treated him like a loser. He'd show her. If he filled up his wallet, she'd have no desire to fall out of line. He stopped in front of the staircase leading upstairs to the bakery and answered the phone.

"Hello?"

"Mumtaz." He didn't recognize the voice on the other line. Whoever it was sounded like they'd swallowed a handful of gravel.

"Yes? Hello?"

"Hey, Mumtaz. It's Chef Anna. How are you?"

"Chef Anna? Do you have a cold or something?" He hoped not. Tomorrow was the day that he promised to haul the rest of her order to the restaurant.

"No, I'm just...tired. Listen, can you get more of this salt?"

"More than what I'm bringing you?"

"Yes."

Mumtaz frowned. What was she trying to pull? Was she repackaging it and selling it to other chefs behind his back?

"Why do you need so much?"

A scratchy laugh came from the other end of the phone, making his skin crawl. "Relax, Mumtaz. You're my favorite importer. I wouldn't do you dirty."

Mumtaz stuck a finger in his ear to drown out the trumpeter's antics in the jazz lounge. "Excuse me, Chef, say that again?"

"Are you fishing for compliments?" she asked. Mumtaz cringed at the sound of her croaky voice and swallowed to clear his own throat.

"No. You said I'm your favorite importer. Last month, you told me I was on the lower end. I'm wondering what brought about your change of heart?"

"Bring me as much salt as you can and you'll be my favorite forever," Chef Dupree said. Mumtaz leaned into his phone and listened. The drum solo made hearing damned near impossible, but if he concentrated, he could hear the faint sound of dry smacking lips.

"Chef? Are you... eating it?"

"I expect my new stock on time. I've already sent the money to your account."

"You did? But we haven't agreed on a price yet."

"Mumtaz, I don't want to argue, okay? What I've sent you should guarantee an exclusive partnership. We'll sign the contracts tomorrow. Don't keep me waiting." The call dropped and Mumtaz cursed. If Chef Anna thought she was going to get away without haggling, she'd lost her mind.

Curiosity overcame him and he swiped open the bank account app on his cellphone. He staggered as he checked and rechecked the numbers. If he added up all the money he'd made in his twenty-eight-year-old life, it might come close to the amount he now had in his account.

He was going to need an attorney and a real accountant who knew about tax shelters. Aminah's brother-in-law, Salman wouldn't cut it. "What the hell is in this salt?"

Chapter Fourteen

Mumtaz loaded heavy bags of salt into a rental truck and stretched his aching back. It felt good to be doing honest work for once. *I'm back, baby.*

Chef Malcolm had done him a favor last night by alluding to a new artisanal salt imported from West Africa in his social media feeds. His enormous fan base started asking questions about the brand and seller, but he played coy. Mumtaz hoped Chef Anna didn't get upset now that she wanted an exclusive deal with him.

She'd been texting him all morning while he loaded the truck. He was happy to see them both sweat. The smart thing to do, of course, was make them both pay. And for what? Grains of salt. Mumtaz couldn't believe Chef Anna paid fifty percent more for this new batch. She happily obliged, filling his bank account with numbers he'd never seen before. Her quick payment left him wondering if he had charged enough in the first place. He shook off the thought and replaced his quizzical expression with a grin.

Things were looking up. Soon, he'd have enough to pay back Luqman. There might even be enough left over to reinvest into the business after he paid his overdue bills. And his bookie. When this was all over, he was going to look for a house in Copperhead Cliffs. Two. He'd buy a house for his mother, and Mo could be as freaky as she pleased in the house next door. Well, maybe down the street.

His excitement had him feeling gracious for once, and thankful. A rare moment of reverence overcame him, and he raised his hands to his ears, then dropped to his knees, prostrating in the direction of Makkah. When he finished, his heart felt lighter, cleaner.

He continued loading the bags of salt, tossing them into the back of the truck. A few grains spilled out into the truck's bed, and he picked up a pinch, sprinkling it onto the palm of his hand. It didn't look like much. Little gray rocks with red and pink granules scattered throughout. Mumtaz lifted his hand to his lips, curious.

At this time in his life, the words amounted to little more than a ritualistic reflex, but he said, "Bismillah," blessing the salt anyway. The grains exploded in his hand the way bang snaps did when he used to throw them at his sister. The chemical reaction stung his fingertips. "What the hell?"

He shook a bag, freeing some of the grains and swiped them up. "Bismillah." Again, the grains detonated in his hand, leaving tiny trails of smoke.

He recalled Mo warning him about the salt's contents. Not edible. His phone beeped in his pocket, and he checked it. Chef Anna again. He dialed into his voicemail and listened to the garbled message. Her words slurred together, making no sense. Either way, he was running late. He closed the truck and got on the road.

"Chef Dupree? Miss Anna, I'm here with your salt." Mumtaz peeked into the restaurant's back door and waited for a beat. The overhead lights flickered off and on like a child playing with the switch.

"Hello?" Mumtaz knocked on the door three times and waited. No answer. Logic dictated that the door wouldn't be unlocked unless someone from the kitchen staff were inside. He expected the little kitchen porter to greet him at the door, but no one came.

He rolled the dolly across the threshold. He'd bring in the first batch, then find out where everyone was hiding. His nose wrinkled at the stench in the air. It reminded him of a backed up septic tank.

"Chef Anna, are you here?" Mumtaz walked through the maze of steaming tables and spotless workstations in the kitchen, expecting to bump into sauciers and sous chefs, or tripping over potato peelings that some grunt spilled onto the terracotta tiled flooring. There was no sign of anyone. Where were they?

Chef Anna's smiling brown face and small blonde locs were nowhere to be found. On a rare occasion, Chef Anna's sous chef, Tomás, would pay him for deliveries if the chef herself didn't have time to see him. Save for the enormous stock pots with boiling water on the back burners of a stove, there was no evidence of another living soul in the kitchen.

"Hello, delivery. It's Mumtaz. Where do you guys want this salt?" The incessant squeak of the dolly wheels bounced off the stainless-steel walls and appliances, echoing throughout the space. Mumtaz made a mental note to spray lubricant on them when he got the chance.

Mumtaz sat the dolly upright and unbuttoned his blazer. Humidity from the rising steam in the center island made the skin on his lower back itchy. He squirmed, rubbing against a handle on the dolly to relieve it.

"Chef Anna? Chef Tomás? Guys, I've got your delivery here. Eight pallets." The sooner they came to get it, the sooner he could get out of here. The stench had grown stronger as he approached the front of the kitchen. Maybe Tomás had a bad batch of meat or something. *They'd better hope the health department isn't in the neighborhood.* In his estimation, the stink alone was worthy of a violation.

A wet, smacking sound drew his attention to the opposite side of the kitchen, near the convection ovens. Mumtaz walked towards it, bumping his hip into a cabinet.

"Damn," he said, rubbing his hip and checking the pocket of his jacket for snags. Frothy, red liquid with bits of meat streamed into the floor drain under his feet. "Yuck. What are you guys doing, butchering meat? I thought you did that in the back room?" *What kind of animal smells like that?* He searched for something to clean the mess from his shoes but ended up shaking his feet like a cat with wet paws.

Mumtaz stepped over a steady stream of black globs and clotted red chunks as he continued towards the other end of the kitchen. The trail of blood led him around the next corner where he found someone standing against the opposite wall.

"Oh, there you are. Sorry, Chef Tomás. I stepped in the mess from your butchered meat—" Mumtaz squinted, uncertain of what he saw in front of him.

Chef Anna knelt with her back to him in front of Chef Tomás. She moved close to his midsection and made little sucking sounds.

"Shit. I'm sorry, I thought you knew I was coming, uh, arriving. What are you guys doing?"

Mortified, Mumtaz glanced at them once again, then dropped his eyes and backed away. What had he walked into? A trail of foamy blood running between his feet caught his attention. His eyes followed it back to the source and Mumtaz jumped backwards, knocking over a stack of gleaming, stainless steel colanders.

Tomás's arm twitched and flicked the light switch on and off. His eyes rolled to the top of his head and white bubbles escaped his weathered lips. The skin around his mouth looked like he'd been outside in extreme heat without water, his tongue bloated.

Mumtaz reassessed the scene. What had appeared to be a carnal act was in fact, carnivorous. Chef Anna had been biting chunks out of his gut and salt crystals, along with chunks of flesh spilled from it.

The crash had caught Chef Anna's attention. Her head turned towards him in jerky movements. She looked wild in the eyes, like a crazed beast. Mumtaz froze, awed by the crystallized blackish liquid spattered across her face. She zeroed in on Mumtaz, edging closer to him. Her body convulsed, and rabid, frothy foam spilled from her mouth, tiny flakes of salt glistening down her bloodied chin.

"Chef?" She snarled at him and bared her teeth. Chef Anna crouched on the floor in front of him and he watched in horror as the woman's backbone grew, widening her shoulders. Her arms elongated and her fingernails pushed out of the nail beds, replaced by longer, sharper claws. "Shit." The flickering light morphed her face into a sinister sneer, contrasting the dead look in her eyes as her thighs widened, bursting her pant legs at the seams.

Mumtaz backed away, glancing at the door, gauging how far he would have to run. It was a long sprint to the other side of the kitchen. The long line of stainless-steel cabinets on either side of the aisle made it look farther.

He watched the short woman from the corner of his eye. Her blood-stained blond locs stuck to her forehead and cheeks. A voice in his head wondered if appealing to her senses would snap her out of whatever trance she had fallen into. Another voice told him how stupid he was for thinking that. *This is no fucking trance; she's a monster!* Still, he had to try something. The door was too far.

"Chef Anna? What's wrong? Do you need medical attention?" The question, pointless and stupid, was directed at the wrong person. After one last flick of the lights, Tomás slid to the floor, plunging them into darkness.

Chef Anna, whose eyes glowed electric blue in the darkness, seemed not to notice. She came charging at Mumtaz full throttle. He yelped and jumped out of her way in the nick of time. She flew past him towards the exit and spun on her heels to face him.

Great. There goes my escape plan.

Chef Anna reared back her head and jerked it back and forth, arching the bony plates of her back through the tattered remains of her chef's coat. Mumtaz wondered if he should grab her and hold her down but hesitated. She appeared a lot stronger than him. She regurgitated, then swallowed something, which he presumed was a piece of Tomás.

Before he could react, Chef Anna was at him again. He pivoted, hopping over Tomás, and ran down the opposite side of the counter. She caught up to him, and her hand found the small of his back. Her claws sank into his jacket.

Mumtaz screamed and stumbled, tripping Chef Anna with his feet. Her legs didn't recover, and she fell face first onto the grill. "Oh, my God! Chef!" Mumtaz approached her, then recoiled. The odor of burning flesh made him retch. She peeled herself off the grill without his assistance and with little remaining of one side of her face. His stomach lurched but Chef Anna didn't react at all.

How was she not bothered by the heat from the grill? And what was she trying to do to him? She charged him again.

Mumtaz feigned left, then right, but she kept up with him, swiping at his clothing. He looked into her eyes, searching for recognition, but Chef Anna wasn't there. Her jaws opened and shut, snapping her elongated teeth.

For a moment, he wondered if he were in another nightmare and his body lay tucked in bed, safe and sound. Chef Anna answered the question with a slash down his chest.

Pain doubled him over and his shirt and blazer soaked with blood. *This is no dream.* Mumtaz regrouped, and his instincts kicked in, pushing him into survival mode. He glanced at the counters in his immediate vicinity, looking for a weapon. *Where are the knives?*

It dawned on him as he pushed a mini-island with a butcher block in between him and the crazed chef that there were none. Chefs brought their own knives to the kitchen.

Mumtaz slid across the floor out of the way of Chef Anna's claws. She was faster than him, pouncing before he could scramble away on his hands and knees. Pain shot through his upper calf as she sliced into it. "Sonofabitch!" His good leg reared back, and he kicked her in the face, freeing himself.

He got to his feet and hobbled towards the door, but she tackled him from behind and they went down, spilling an assortment of spoons and ladles to the floor with them. He flipped over and shoved the wooden handle of a spoon into her mouth, and she bit into it. The spoon splintered and fell away in pieces.

He grabbed her forehead to keep her teeth from sinking into his flesh, but there was nothing he could do about her nails. She thrashed on top of him, cutting and digging into the forearms of his jacket. Lifting his hips, he bore down on the floor with both feet, despite the pain. He tried sliding out from under her, but she held on.

Flecks of blood dripped into his eyes from his arms, blinding him. Mumtaz reached out for anything that would help him escape. The harder he reached, the more his clumsy fingers pushed everything away.

Mumtaz jerked and bucked his hips, flopping closer to the station nearest him. A hard swipe of her hand cut down his wrist, dangerously close to the artery, reddening his sleeves.

He grabbed the long, stainless-steel handle of a soup ladle, gripping it until his fingers hurt. With his other hand, he lifted her chin, then brought down the ladle down hard, bashing her head. Mumtaz beat her until he split the meat open, exposing the white of her skull. Chef Anna didn't flinch. It took all his will to hit her again. And again. Unperturbed, she backed up and launched herself at him.

Mumtaz bent his legs, catching her with his feet. He kicked with considerable force, throwing her across the kitchen. When she landed, her limbs shot out, stiffened, then dropped. She stood there, motionless. He didn't dare approach until her eyes closed and her head slumped.

Mumtaz gripped the ladle and moved closer. *She's out for the count.* He used it to move her head out of the way and assess the damage. It was hard to see with all the lights out, save for the emergency lights and the red exit sign at the back, but he couldn't miss the thick, wooden broom handle protruding from her chest. *Right through the heart.*

Life was over for Chef Anna. He tossed the ladle onto a nearby counter and made haste towards the kitchen entrance. Poor Tomás needed medical attention right away. Mumtaz hurried to the area where the chef had been pinned to the wall, helpless against Chef Anna. Mumtaz rounded the corner and stopped dead in his tracks. Tomás was gone.

Chapter Fifteen

"SLOW DOWN, Taz. What do you mean, she's dead? Who's dead?"

"Chef Anna. She came at me, Jasim. She was eating Tomás, crazy cannibal style. I kicked her off me, and now she's impaled on a fucking broom. What am I going to do, man? They'll give me a lethal injection for this."

"Did you have a nightmare again? Maybe you should take a deep breath and wake up."

"I am awake, dammit, you're not listening." Mumtaz paced back and forth in the kitchen of Dupree's, trying to make sense of the last few minutes. His first instinct was to call Jasim. He'd have been better off calling a total stranger for all the good it had done.

"Okay. Let's say that what you're saying is true. Chef Anna Dupree turned into a psycho killer with claws and sharp teeth and ate Chef Tomás."

"She took some bites out of him."

"Right.... Now, you said a broom handle impaled her?"

"Correct. It went right through her, from back to front."

"And now, Chef Tomás is gone from the kitchen."

"Yes."

"Did you look for him?"

"No."

"Why not?"

"Are you crazy? I want to wipe my prints off everything and get out of here."

"Don't you think the man needs your help?"

Mumtaz sighed. "Yeah, I guess. No, you're right, Jasim. I should help him. It's impossible to wipe all my prints anyway. Besides, they'll find my DNA too. Do you know that she sliced right through my good jacket? And I'm gonna need stitches all over the place."

"Boo hoo for your copycat designer clothes. Go find the man. If he's able to speak, he can corroborate your story to the police. Personally, I think you're tripping. If not, I'll see you on the news. Peace out, homie." Jasim ended the call and Mumtaz chucked the phone into his pocket.

He winced as he peeled the layers of clothing away from the wounds on his chest and applied anti-bacterial spray from a first aid kit he found on the wall. The wound at the small of his back could wait for now.

A crash in the dining room sent a chill down Mumtaz's spine. Deep, guttural growls rumbled on the other side of the swinging door. A sinking feeling told him that Chef Tomás had the crazies like Chef Anna. He couldn't leave him out there for the staff to find on Tuesday.

What if he tried to kill them? *What if he tries to kill me?* Maybe it would be better to slip out the window of Chef Anna's office and call it a day.

Mumtaz grabbed the bloody ladle and approached the swinging door with caution. If Chef Tomás needed help, he would do what he could. If he behaved the way Chef Anna had, he hoped there was something useful to fend him off in the dining room.

Mumtaz peeked through the porthole, hoping to spot him. The dining room lights were off and moving shadows from the trees outside made it seem like the man was everywhere and nowhere at the same time. Mumtaz pushed open the door a little and peeked into the dining room.

He uttered a curse under his breath, unsure what to do. The searing waves of pain in his chest reminded Mumtaz that he needed medical attention. Whatever he did, he had to hurry.

His mind wouldn't let him forget how Chef Anna had been feasting on the man. The smacking sound from her mouth replayed on an endless loop in his head. Maybe Tomás was laying on the floor somewhere in need of medical attention. He couldn't be sure without checking out the dining area.

A glass sculpture on the opposite side of the room collapsed. Mumtaz looked behind him. Should he run out the back, escaping this hellish nightmare or stay here and clean up this mess.? It was now or never. Mumtaz tightened his grip on the ladle and stole out of the kitchen. He might be a terrible businessman, but he was no coward.

~

MUMTAZ STEPPED into the dining room, crunching over the fragments of broken candle sconces and shattered glass partitions littering the floor. The man had run through here like a bull. In the far corner, a shadow sprang out from the dark. The chef landed on a table and Mumtaz hit the floor behind the host table.

A mess of red linen, darkened and soaked through with blood covered the floor. The chef must have sought help when he initially slipped into the dining room, but he was not the same man now.

Mumtaz saw him reflected in the mirror above the bar, holding something between his fingers, licking it like a starved animal. It was a saltshaker. Chef Tomás grimaced from the taste and threw the shaker, cracking the mirror. He moved on to the next table, licked the shaker and threw that one too.

Mumtaz took his chance, creeping out from behind the host table. With Chef Tomás facing the opposite direction, he wound up the over-sized soup spoon like he was at home plate with bases loaded and cracked the chef across the back of his skull. They both froze in place. An eerie quiet settled over the restaurant. The back of the chef's head pulsed as his backbone cracked and widened like Chef Anna's had. Mumtaz watched with horror as the vertebral column grew out from the chef's spine in bony spikes. He knew then that he had messed up.

Mumtaz winced as the chef faced him. He saw the same electric glow in his eyes without a hint of humanity. This had been a big mistake.

He took a deep breath and stumbled backwards into a table with empty wine glasses, knocking the entire place setting to the floor. The crash spurred him on, and Mumtaz ran for his life. Chef Tomás was on him, slashing at his body.

Mumtaz cried out as the demonic man widened the gash in the small of his back. He had to get him off or die trying. Mumtaz grabbed hold of a shard of glass and twisted himself to stick it wherever he could.

He lodged it into the meaty part of the chef's thigh to no avail. Mumtaz bucked, knocking Chef Tomás off him, and got to his feet. He scrambled over tables and chairs, clambered over the leather booths until he reached the swinging doors, crashing into the kitchen.

The chef stayed hot on his heels. Mumtaz turned corners, looking for a way out. He leaped a countertop, soaring to the other side of the room. Chef Tomás hopped it without effort, missing Mumtaz by mere inches.

Mumtaz bypassed the empty slaughter room. There was no way in hell he was going in there. He ran to the freezer, yanking open the door and slamming it in the nick of time. Chef Tomás tore at it from outside. The crazed growls and scratching noises made Mumtaz's blood run cold, but for now, the two remained separated.

The bastard can't open the door. Think. THINK!

Mumtaz scanned the freezer, hoping to come up with a plan. The room had racks stacked with produce on one side, meat on the other, and dairy products in the back. A loud bang came from outside, matching the thumping in Mumtaz's chest. Chef Tomás wanted in.

Mumtaz got to work. He tired himself out emptying vacuum-sealed hunks of beef from their storage racks, but the ghastly noises from outside spurred him on. Once emptied, the racks pulled away from the walls with little effort. He had one shot to get this right.

Mumtaz slid the first racks against the door, lining them up into two rows with enough space left in the middle to run through. He twisted off the cap of an orange soda bottle, pouring the fizzy beverage all over the thin steel floor, then climbed to the top of the first set of racks and kicked the door to open it. It didn't budge. "Move, dumbass." Chef Tomás growled and banged the door in reply. Mumtaz sighed and kicked again.

The chef responded by banging against the door even harder. Mumtaz caught glimpses of the grayish-black flesh of his face as the incessant hits released the air-tight seal, popping the door open a few inches between blows.

The harder he slammed against it, the worse the layers of his forehead cracked and bled. Mumtaz climbed down from the rack and waited until the chef bashed his head into the door, then gave it a healthy kick. The door flew open, and Chef Tomás landed on his backside for a split second, hopping onto his feet faster than Mumtaz expected.

The swift recovery and odd way the chef chomped his teeth scared the shit out of him. But it was the way he stared at him that nearly broke Mumtaz's spirit. If he fucked this up, he could kiss his miserable life goodbye.

Chef Tomás dropped his hands to his sides and watched Mumtaz like he had all the time in the world. And maybe he did; nothing sat between them now. *Maybe I'm a dumbass. Why the hell did I open the door? I've handed myself to this freak on a platter.*

Mumtaz buttoned his blazer, careful not to disturb the deep gashes in his middle. The last thing he wanted was for it to get caught on something. The chef tilted his head and sniffed at the cold air blowing out from the back of the freezer, picking up the scent of Mumtaz's bloody and battered body. Fresh meat.

Mumtaz took a deep breath and tried clearing his mind. *You have to survive. For the baby.* He pictured what he had to do and waited for Chef Tomás to make the first move. If he failed, it was game over. For his sake, he hoped things transpired with haste if he did.

"A'uthu bikalimaatil-laahit-taammaati min sharri maa khalaqa." The long-forgotten prayer to ward off evil stumbled out of his mouth without effort. There was nothing like the threat of death to awaken the unused portions of the memory.

Mumtaz focused, homing in on the chef's predatory stare. He loosened his tight fists, shaking out the tension. He dropped them to his sides, and they twitched in anticipation. This was going to be a hell of a ride.

A timer near the boiling pots went off. Mumtaz turned towards the noise for a split second. Chef Tomás did not.

With a scuttle of sneakered feet, the chef was off and running. Mumtaz bent his legs, keeping them fluid as Chef Tomás came for him, arms, and razor-sharp nails flailing. Mumtaz held his position, hoping to God this worked.

The chef's black sneaker touched the ramp leading into the walk-in freezer and seconds later, he launched himself off it like a diver on a springboard. He was no athlete, but Mumtaz used the last good amount of strength and agility he had, vaulting himself onto the top of the left-hand racks.

Chef Tomás took a swipe at him but missed as he slid further into the freezer, feet squeaking in the spilled orange soda. He hit the floor hard, slamming into the ramp on the back wall.

Mumtaz jumped down from the rack and escaped the freezer before the maniacal chef could recover and come after him. He slammed the door shut and locked it with the key. Chef Tomás banged on the door from the inside, but the lock held.

"Yes! Mumtaz, you silly jackass, you did it!" He leaned against the freezer door, arms still raised in victory, and sobbed.

CRASHES from inside the freezer prompted Mumtaz to jump off the counter. He took his time searching the kitchen from top to bottom. There had to be something. Mumtaz found kitchen tongs and cutlery in the dishwashing area that he'd missed earlier. A steak knife would have to do.

He walked towards the dining room door and glanced across the hall. He hadn't noticed that Chef Anna's office door was open when he walked past here before. The office looked trashed. He had to step over torn bags of salt to get inside. His shoes made crunching sounds as he walked over mounds of it.

Piles of discarded granules sat on her desk, on the chair, and all over the floor. "Damn." Some of the white powder had streaks of blood in it.

Mumtaz crouched to look at the salt. It didn't look any different from ordinary table salt, nor did it have an odor. He wasn't sure if salt could spoil. The closer he got to it, the stronger his urge to taste it, as if some invisible forces were coercing him. The continuous guttural growls coming from Chef Tomás in the freezer snapped him out of the trance. He wiped the drooling corners of his mouth and backed away.

He examined the desk, wondering how things could have gotten out of control like this. Maybe it wasn't the salt. Maybe they had taken some weird concoction of illicit drugs and they turned psycho.

Mumtaz remembered seeing a man high on PCP once. The man dislocated his own shoulders to slide out of the handcuffs a police officer had slipped on him during a protest downtown. He tore the skin off his wrists to free himself, then popped his shoulders back into the sockets and escaped.

If the cops showed up, they wouldn't care about salt. They would care about the dead woman in the kitchen and blame him for her death. Mumtaz backed away from Chef Anna's desk and looked around the sparse office.

There were unopened boxes stacked next to an empty bookcase and samples of table linens strewn about a chaise in the corner. The place hadn't even had its grand opening yet, and the owner lay dead in her own kitchen. A blue leather tote bag sitting on a file cabinet caught his eye.

He'd seen Chef Anna baby that leather bag many times, wiping it down after resting it on the floor, making sure it didn't get wet as she walked through the kitchen. Mumtaz wondered if there was someone he should call to break the bad news. If there was, they deserved to hear it from him, not the police. Curiosity won him over and Mumtaz walked over and opened it.

Chef Tomás continued banging on the door reminding him of his unfinished business in the freezer. Mumtaz ignored it as his hands swept around inside the satchel. Maybe Chef Anna kept her knife bag inside.

His cellphone rang in his pocket, shooting his blood pressure through the roof. He checked the display but didn't recognize the number.

"Hello?" he cradled the phone between his cheek and shoulder, leaving his hands free to rummage in her bag.

"Hey, did you get the you-know-what for you-know-who?" Mumtaz paused, trying to place the voice of the idiot on the other end of the phone.

"What? Who the hell is this?" If his hands were free, he would have hung up. Instead, he busied himself with the zipper of a bank deposit bag. The woman carried everything in this tote. Except her knives, of course.

"This is Hamza."

"Hamza who? You think you're the only Muslim in town with the name Hamza? Be specific." He unzipped the money bag and stuck his hand inside. Empty. Mumtaz tossed it aside and shook his head.

His eyes darted around, scanning the office. The sun broke through the clouds and the gleam of a half-open wall safe caught his eye. The cash stacked inside almost made him wet himself.

"It's Hamza Rahmaninov."

"Who?" Mumtaz made his way to the safe and opened the door all the way. Except for one chunk, the entire safe was filled to the brim with cash.

"Lucky Luke's cousin, you dick."

"Oh. Why didn't you say so?" he asked, irritated.

"Didn't you hear me? I'm Lucky Luke's—"

"Yeah, I heard you. You're a nobody, trying to scare me by using your cousin's reputation, which tells me all that I need to know about you."

"Listen—"

"No, you listen," Mumtaz said, adjusting the phone to get a better grip on a brick of hundreds. "Tell your boss that I have his money. All of it." Mumtaz laughed.

"Bullshit."

"Don't be a hater, Hamza."

"Trust me, there's no hate. But I know a loser like you doesn't get their hands on that kind of money from honest work."

"Then it's a good thing Luqman isn't running a background check and asking for receipts, isn't it? Now, be a good little boy and tell your cousin to meet me at midnight. I'll be in the parking lot of Andalusia, in Hillstead Village."

"Don't be late," Hamza said with a slight edge.

"I'll be early," Mumtaz said, hanging up. *But for now, I've got some good cheer to spread around.* Things were looking up. He visualized the curse shifting away from his family and the look on his mother's face when he bought her a new car and showered her with gifts.

He'd buy the warehouse from her, relieving her of the debts she owed on his behalf. Of course, he couldn't forget his boy, Jasim. He'd give Mo enough money to whet her appetite. Then, he'd hunt for a new car and kiss his Toyota goodbye.

Chef Tomás let out a blood-curdling howl in the freezer and Mumtaz's fantasy collapsed. He needed to patch himself up and find a sufficient way to dispatch the chef. For now, he was going to pack the money and take care of Luqman. "I'm coming back for you, Tomás. God willing."

Chapter Sixteen

"Were you in a car accident or a knife fight?" Mumtaz's mother frowned at her son who sat at the head of the dining table in her seat.

"Accident," Mumtaz said, counting cash. After he got off the phone with Hamza, he thought long and hard about Chef Anna. She lived alone and had no close relatives or romantic partner as far as he knew. A wave of guilt washed over him. She had no one to mourn her. He convinced himself that he was all she had. *I was like a son to her.* She would want him to empty the entire safe and bring the cash home. No use in it going to waste.

"If you got into an accident, why does your car look unharmed?"

"Ma, I don't feel like talking right now. I've got a lot on my mind."

"A lot on your mind? You've got a lot on my table, too," she said, raising a balled fist to her wide hips. "Mumtaz, look me in the eye and tell me where you got all this money, boy. Did it come from your Voodoo girl?" His mother poked at the bricks of cash on the table with the tip of her cane.

He paused scribbling figures in his notebook and looked at his mother. "Hoodoo, and no, it didn't. Chef Anna Dupree and I are in business. She drew up a contract today." That part was true. He'd discovered it in the safe. His mother didn't need to know that Chef Anna had signed it, but they hadn't gotten around to discussing it, or the gruesome reasons why. She scrutinized the endless piles of money stacked across the dining table and shook her head.

"Does Hidaya know about this?"

Mumtaz shrugged. "Hidaya is not privy to what happens in my business. Besides, what's there to know?"

"There's a lot to know, Mumtaz. Don't you think she'd like to know that you made it big and have spread money all over the dining room?"

"No. Hidaya doesn't know, and I'd like to keep it that way for now."

"How come?"

"Because she's nosy and likes to jump to higher conclusions than you do. I don't feel like dealing with her right now, I have a lot of debts to clear." He scribbled something on his paper then tucked the pencil behind his ear.

"Are the police going to come searching for all of this?"

"No, Ma. I made this money because I was in the right place at the right time."

"Oh, my God. You're a drug dealer. What did I tell you about those boys on the corner?"

"I'm not a drug dealer, Ma. I am an importer of fine foods like I've always been. We have Mo to thank for our new fortune."

"Aha, I knew it. What did that girl give you, Mumtaz? Is she the head of a cartel or something?"

"Relax, Ma. Monet and I are selling salt."

His mother rolled her eyes. "Ya, Allah, where did I go wrong, raising such a liar? We can't keep this dirty money, Mumtaz. Take it back." She spat at it and pushed it away from her side of the table.

"Ma, knock it off, I'm counting over here," Mumtaz said, catching bills before they hit the floor. "And I'm not taking it back. This money was meant for me. It's fate. Look at this." He handed her the contract that he found in the safe wedged between stacks of cash that, from the looks of it, Chef Anna had drawn up in haste.

"Did you forge this contract?" She held it up and moved it back and forth in front of her face until her eyes adjusted.

"Ma, seriously, what do you think of your son? No, I didn't. This is legitimate. Be proud of me. I did something right for once."

"Like last night, when you brought that witch into my home?"

"Mo's more of a con artist than a real witch, Ma."

"And you have no business mixing with her, witch, or no witch. She's not your wife, son. She's probably someone else's wife." His mother's voice raised to a shriek. "How could you associate with such a person after what our family went through in Mali? They ruined us, Mumtaz. Your poor auntie and every male in the family, except you and your cousin Abdullah have died because of black magic. Did she conjure this for you too?" She shook her cane at the money.

"No, she did not conjure it for me. I earned it."

She screwed up her face and studied her son. "Habibi, my dear son. I was not born yesterday. Whatever you have done to cover my dining table with this money was haraam." His mother grunted and used her cane to coax her knees to stand. "Fix it, Mumtaz. And get this out of here. I never want to see it again."

Mumtaz ignored her so he wouldn't lose count.

"By the way, I'm going to your sister's house. We might swing by Aminah's house for dinner, so you'll have to fend for yourself. A twenty-eight-year-old man should be able to cook from time to time, don't you think?"

"Oh, Ma. You're making me lose count." He tapped the remote control and turned on the television in the living room. The news came on and his mother frowned. She hated watching the news.

"I can take a hint, ungrateful boy." She walked to the foyer to put on her shoes. Mumtaz stopped counting and ran to the door.

"Ma, wait." He caught up as she slipped her left foot into her shoe.

"What is it, Mumtaz? Am I not moving fast enough for—" She grew quiet and still as he held her close.

They stood in silence and Mumtaz stilled his mind, recalling all the times he'd given her grief and heartache surfaced. He wanted to apologize for being a difficult son, but he kept quiet, lest his mouth betray him with a hundred insufficient words.

"I love you, Ma." Mumtaz rested his chin on her head. Tears from sorrow and hurt fell from his eyes and spread across the top of her hijab. His mother gave him an extra squeeze and he shuddered from the pain in his back.

"I love you too, habibi."

He drew back from her and took in the mixed expression of love and confusion on her face. A shy smile spread across her lips as she picked up her handbag. "I have to go. Your sister's waiting."

"I know," he said, opening the door for her. "Make du'a for me. Ask Allah for my forgiveness," he said.

"InshaAllah," his mother said, stepping across the threshold. Mumtaz watched her grasp the porch handrail and make her way to the pavement.

"Things are looking up, Ma. I'm going to take care of everything." His mother paused without turning back, then kept walking. Mumtaz thought he saw her wipe her eyes.

AN HOUR LATER, he recounted the money. There was no time left to waste. It was easier with his mother gone, although his heart ached, now that he sat alone in the house.

He tallied and divided the large amount of cash into enough for everyone in the family who lived in Rosewood Hollow. He trembled as he placed Abdullah's portion into an envelope, specifying that it be sent to him in Mali.

He closed the last envelope addressed to his baby cousin, Aminah, then stacked two smaller portions on the table, ignoring the way his hands shook. The longer he waited to take care of Chef Tomás, the more nervous he became. Now that he was away from the restaurant, he dreaded unlocking the freezer door and dispatching of the crazed man.

The alternative was to leave him inside and let someone else find him. He could make an anonymous phone call to the police. After all, cops had plenty of guns.

But what if they saw his prints on everything? He attempted to wipe the place clean, but every surface was stainless steel and glass, and there was no telling what he missed. He didn't want to go to jail.

On the other hand, if he did nothing, someone from the restaurant staff might open the freezer and find a nasty surprise waiting inside. There was no way around it. Mumtaz had to take care of the situation.

The question was, how? He needed to do it quickly, without losing the element of surprise. The chef's movements had been fast and unnatural, and he seemed impervious to pain. He couldn't go back there. Chef Tomás would rip him apart.

I have to tell Mo. She'd be pissed, but he had to confess that he'd touched her salt without her permission. Maybe she knew how to save the man, or maybe she could whip up a spell to stop whatever instinct had him acting like a madman.

He rose from the table, put the smaller bills into an envelope, then grabbed a large envelope with Luqman's name scrawled across the front and left the house. It was eight o'clock in the evening and the car dealerships would close soon.

"ARE you sure about taking it without a test drive?" The first stop on Mumtaz's list was the used car dealership. He had passed by here many times on his way to the importer markets in the early morning, admiring the new vehicles. Today, he decided frugality was a virtue and bought a used one with cash. If he was going to die, he would at least do it in style.

"I'm sure, Abu Idris. I'll take it." Mumtaz sat behind the wheel of his new, used white Ford Bronco and watched with satisfaction as one of the car detailers turned over the engine in his Celica. "I just want to get as far away from that lemon as I can," he said.

"Sounds good to me. If you're unsatisfied for any reason, give me a call. My number is on the card."

"Absolutely," Mumtaz said, watching the detailer drive away. He cracked a smile and bid the old clunker adieu. A slight twinge of sadness hit him in the depths of his chest. The old girl had been moody as hell in the winter and unrelenting in the summer heat, but she'd been there when he lost his Bimmer.

"In the last fifteen years. I've never had someone come in here and drop ten thousand on a car that they didn't test drive or take to a mechanic," the dealer said. "You're not going to rob a bank, are you?" He followed up the question with a hearty laugh. "But I suppose, if you were going to rob a bank, you may as well steal the car too."

Mumtaz offered a weak smile and held out his hand. "Shukran for your help, brother, I appreciate it. I'll call you if there's any trouble, but I don't think you'll hear from me again."

"Thank you for your business, Brother Mumtaz. Enjoy the car." The dealer returned Mumtaz's handshake and backed up from the vehicle. "As Salaamu Alaikum."

"Wa Alaikum As Salaam," Mumtaz said, grinning. He glanced at the rearview mirror and saw the detailer walking into the garage. The old Celica was gone.

Mumtaz merged onto the highway, sinking the pedal into the floorboards. If a million cops pulled him over tonight, he didn't care. A smile cracked his lips as he took in the irony of a Black man being pulled over by the police in a white Ford Bronco. He had a couple of stops to make before he met his fate at Dupree's.

"Wow, look at you, driving your new whip. I can't believe you finally bought a new car." Monet pushed her sunglasses onto the top of her head and circled the Ford. It was nine-forty and Mumtaz had pulled up to the curb the moment she walked out the doors of the Crystal Falls Mall. Mumtaz unlocked his new vehicle and held out his hand to assist her.

"Get in, we'll go for a spin around the block."

"I can't. Someone is supposed to pick me up."

"Let me guess. That cop is still sniffing around. I'm tired of you hanging onto this guy like he's ever gonna take you back, Mo. You believe in fate, don't you? If the two of you were meant to be, he would have taken you back when his wife died. Better still, he would have gotten you pregnant, not me."

"Listen, Taz, you don't understand. Norman and I are bonded with magic. That's deeper than any physical relationship. He'll always be a part of my life, whether you like it or not."

"Well, you and I are bonded with our baby and this." He opened an envelope full of cash and her eyes grew wide.

"Is that what I think it is?" she asked.

"Yes, now get in the car and let's go."

"Are you gonna tell me where you got all this cash? And don't tell me any bullshit, like you got it selling golden steaks or caviar-stuffed snake brains," Monet said. She folded her legs under her and waited for an explanation. The green light from the sushi restaurant across from her apartment glowed on the side of her face.

He held up his hand, exposing his palm. "Okay, this is probably going to make you mad."

"Oh, shit. The lines. They're all gone." Monet clambered out of the chair and sat on the bed to get a closer look. "I know a conjuring woman from Nigeria, maybe she can help us."

Mumtaz shook his head. "Forget it. There's no need."

"We have to try. She's good at spell work and she knows all about curses."

"Stop, Mo."

"I tried calling her late last night, but she was out of town at a seance. She should be back by now."

"There's no time."

"Taz, please, let me—"

"I sold some of your salt to Chef Anna Dupree and... oh, baby, it's bad."

Monet reared back. The freckles on her brown face grew darker. "What the fuck did you say?"

"I'm sorry. I know you told me not to."

"You're sorry? Taz, have you lost your mind? Please tell me no one ate it." He averted his eyes. "You fucking idiot. I told you that salt is not edible. Do you know what happens to people who consume it?"

"Yeah, Mo, I do. That's what I'm trying to tell you."

"You let that chef eat it? Taz, she could have killed half the city by now. That salt is full of jinn spirits. They take over the body, and I don't know what they do, but it spreads, and people die."

"I've seen what they do, and it's not pretty," he said.

"Well, where is this Chef Anna right now? Oh, God, what if she got out?" Monet turned on the television with the remote.

"She didn't get out," Mumtaz said. "What are you doing?"

"I'm checking for news of an outbreak."

"She didn't get out, Mo."

"How can you be sure? Lebe's gonna have our asses for this. There are rules about this stuff, Taz. You can't let uncontrolled magic get loose." She continued flicking through the channels.

"I know she didn't get out because I killed her."

Monet sneered. "No, you didn't."

"I did so."

"You don't have the balls."

"Excuse me? If you think so lowly of me, why are you with me?"

"Why do you think I'm with you? Your sole purpose is to make Norman jealous. I mean, how much value do you think you bring to my life, Taz? You're broke, you live with your mother. You're judgmental, and come from a puritanical Muslim family, and you're not even good at that. You've got nothing going for you. Your bitch-ass couldn't kill anybody. And now I've got to call in the cavalry to clean up your fucking mess."

She reached for her cellphone on the coffee table and dialed a number. He watched her punch in a code and press pound. An automated voice said something he couldn't make out and his mind raced. Who was she calling? Mumtaz thought over the options and snatched the phone.

"Give it to me," she said, gnashing her teeth. She reached out and slapped him.

"You're not calling that cop." He opened the balcony door and threw it as far as he could. They watched it hit the ground across the street and smash into a handful of pieces.

"You stupid sonofabitch. Who's gonna help us now, Taz?"

"I don't need help. If you weren't having my child, this would be the last time you saw me."

"Then say goodbye. I got an abortion."

His mouth fell open. "What?"

"It's gone. And you can be too for all I care."

He looked at her in stunned silence. She returned his stare. "You're lying, right?"

"Nope."

"When could you have gotten an abortion?"

"Maybe it was the day you decided to go behind my back and sell my fucking salt."

"I've heard enough," he said, putting on his jacket.

"Where are you going? Taz? You can't just walk out of here without talking about this. Lebe's gonna have our heads for this."

"Was it even mine?"

She jerked her head and shot him a look of disbelief. "Are you really asking me that right now? Norman and I haven't been together in a long time. It was yours, idiot."

Mumtaz threw his hands in the air. "What do I know?" He reached into his pocket and pulled out his ringing cellphone. "Hello?"

"Taz? This is Malcolm."

"Malcolm? Oh, right, Chef Malcolm. It's kind of a bad time. Can I call you back?"

"You won't believe how long it took me to find your number. I didn't realize Taz was short for Mumtaz," he said. "I tore apart the rolodex looking for you."

"Yes, that's my full name. Listen, Chef, I've got your number, let me get back to you," Mumtaz said, standing. "I've got some important business right now."

"I'm sorry, Taz, but it's imperative that we talk. I need more salt, Taz. The others, they've eaten almost all of it. I have to have more," Chef Malcolm said. Dread washed over him, and he gripped the door frame, waiting for the room to stop spinning.

"What's wrong?" Monet asked.

He shook his head and waved her away. "Chef, where are the others?" His voice cracked and the question came out in a high-pitched squeak.

"Don't know. We were prepping and they started fighting over the salt. Things got aggressive and somebody got hurt. I took the rest of it and locked myself in our steak locker with it. They were pretty pissed off, banging on the door and whatnot. I told them I'd call you and have you bring more bags and they calmed down."

Mumtaz grabbed his keys and held up a finger to Mo. "Is the restaurant open, Chef?"

"No. We closed an hour ago."

"Did you serve the salt to your customers?"

"Can you deliver more of it tonight? We're going to be here for a while. The kitchen's a mess after all the fighting, and—"

"Goddammit, listen to me! Did you serve the salt to your customers?"

"No. I kept it for myself but that nosy bastard, Eduardo, got his hands on it. He thought it was coke, can you believe that? Snorted it and passed it around, then crawled under the cabinets and wouldn't come out."

"Is he alive?"

"Who knows? I don't know where the other two are, but I'm staying in here for now. I can't trust that bitch, Rosie, and Tampa does everything she says. I'm staying put. How soon can you get here?"

Mumtaz grabbed Mo by the hand and led her to the door.

"Taz, what's happening? What the fuck is going on?"

"It's been real, you selfish bitch," he said, planting a kiss on her lips. He reached into the envelope in his pocket and took out the wadded bills of cash, tossing them on the floor. "For your salt."

Mumtaz drew back from her and watched her squat to pick up the bills. She wasn't as pretty as she used to be. He didn't blame what she'd done to the baby on the curse. This relationship was one of his many mistakes. He would take care of each and every other one tonight.

Chapter Seventeen

"Jas, do you still have that piece that you bought a couple of years ago?" Mumtaz took a drink from the cold bottle of lemonade Jasim's wife, Naya had given him while barely disguising her disgust. When Jasim quickly ushered Mumtaz into the backyard in the screened gazebo tent, he suspected his friend had blabbed everything to her. When he saw her staring at them from the kitchen window, he knew.

Jasim eyed Mumtaz with suspicion. "The only reason you'd ask for my gun is if you're short the money you owe Lucky Luke. Man, you could have given me a heads up. I would have left town by now." Jasim wrung his hands together then massaged the fingers, one by one.

"Relax, Jas, I've got the money."

Jasim's hands froze. "Say what?"

Mumtaz nodded. "I got the money and then some."

"Are you serious? Don't play, Taz. Now is not the time for jokes."

"It's no joke. Take a look." He opened the fat envelope he had brought with him and let Jasim peek at the money.

"Oh, my God. Mumtaz, you came through. I thought for sure my life was over."

"Come on, I can't believe you doubted me."

"Never again, homie. Never again." Jasim shook Mumtaz's hand and leaned in for a one-armed hug and brisk pat on the back.

They sat in silence for a few moments, basking in victory. Jasim took a swig from his lemonade, stopped mid sip, pulling his lips from the bottle with a thick sucking sound. "If you've got the money, what the hell do you need my gun for?"

"It's complicated."

"Aw, man, get out of here with that noise, Mumtaz. People need guns to kill other people. Who are you trying to kill?"

"No one."

"Bullshit."

"I swear to you, I'm not trying to kill a human being."

"Say, 'Wallahi.'"

"Seriously? Come on, man, you know I don't like doing that."

"Why not? If you're telling the truth, it shouldn't be a problem. Swear by Allah that you're not killing a person."

"Come on, Jas."

"Do it."

Mumtaz sighed and shook his head. "Wallahi, I'm not going to kill a person with your gun."

Jasim scratched the tight coily hair on his beard as he studied Mumtaz. "Is Mo's man coming after you?"

"Mo and I are through. You were right about her."

"For real? Mumtaz, I'm starting to feel proud of you and hopeful for your future, lad. What have you been up to this week?"

Mumtaz finished off his lemonade and sat the bottle next to his feet. "Too much, Jas. So, can I have it or what?"

"How much ammo do you need for this non-human target?" Jasim opened the zippers on his range bag.

"How much do you have?"

Jasim frowned. "Man... It's like I said before. You do things and the people closest to you get hurt. I sure as hell don't want to go to prison because I gave you my gun."

"Please, Jas. It's life or death."

"No shit."

"I mean it. It's the only way I can stay alive. If things go sour, you should report it stolen, okay?"

"How many magazines do you want?"

"I need them all."

Jasim gave his friend a long, hard look, then shook his head. "Fine. Which one do you want, the seventeen or the nineteen?"

"I'll take the nineteen," Mumtaz said. Jasim slipped the other Glock into a different bag and locked it. "What time is it, Jas?"

"Ten thirty-four. This doesn't feel right to me, man. Do you want me to come with you? Two heads are better than one." He laid a hand on Mumtaz's shoulder and looked him in the eyes. "It seems like you need me to be around more often. You get into a lot of trouble on your own," Jasim said.

"Thanks for the offer, but no thanks. You're right. I've gotten into something heavy, but there's no way that I'm dragging you into it this time. You're a good friend to offer, though. Stupid, but good. I love you, brother." Mumtaz held out his hand to shake and Jasim pulled him close in a bear hug.

"I love you too, man. If you won't let me go with you, what should I do?"

"Walk me to the door, you loyal motherfucker."

THEY HEADED into the house and down the hall, past the living room where Naya and Jasim's mother-in-law prayed 'Isha, then out the front door.

"I cannot believe you bought a fucking Ford Bronco, Taz," Jasim said, climbing into the passenger seat.

"You know I had to do it." Mumtaz chuckled but it sounded flat.

"Chef Anna must have given you a hell of an advance," Jasim said, playing with the visor and opening the glove box.

"She did. Oh, that reminds me. I wanted to tell you something."

"What?"

"You married a good woman. You should listen to her more. She's right a lot of the time."

"You must really be in trouble if you're complimenting Naya. What's gotten into you?" Jasim asked, leaning into the seats.

"Nothing. I'm just doing a lot of reflecting on my life today."

"Damn. Do you have an incurable disease or something?"

"Just an incurable curse," Mumtaz said.

"Don't start that again," Jasim shook his head. "I have to admit, I was skeptical, but this is nice, Taz. Congratulations."

"Thanks. I meant what I said. You married a good woman. Look after her. Other people wish they had a good woman to come home to. Thank Allah that you've got her."

"Alright, mister sappy, I hear you," Jasim said through nervous laughter. The porch light came on and they turned to see Naya glaring at them through the curtain.

"I guess that's your cue."

"Yeah, I gotta go," Jasim said, opening the door and climbing out.

Mumtaz started the vehicle and rolled down the window. "Before you go," Mumtaz said, taking a fat envelope out of his pocket, "I need to give you this."

"What is it?" Jasim asked.

"I forgot to give it to you before your honeymoon," Mumtaz said. Jasim took the envelope and opened it. Mumtaz drove away and turned off his cellphone before he could say anything.

Chapter Eighteen

To Mumtaz's dismay, the ride to Dupree's Restaurant took no time at all. His stomach twisted into knots and the wounds on his back and belly had stiffened, hardening into zipper-like scabs.

He drove around the restaurant twice, making sure no one had stumbled upon the scene and called the police. The place looked deserted, as did the rest of the brick buildings in the area. An occasional couple or single person wandered down the sidewalks, but no one bothered to look into the darkened windows.

Mumtaz climbed out of his truck with the range bag Jasim had given him. He left the doors unlocked for ease of getaway. Once he crossed the street, he stepped into the long alleyway between Dupree's and a gourmet cheese shop.

Although a heavy blanket of humid air settled in the atmosphere and thunder rolled in the distance, Mumtaz shivered. He hoped the tornado watch in the forecast was accurate. It would be nice if it touched down on the restaurant's roof and did the job for him.

The human population was scarce, but the night still jumped with life. Scroungy-looking cats digging in trash bins made him wary. A couple of healthy rats sized him up before finding something else for a snack. After hours, this place gave him the creeps. But none of that was as unsettling as what was inside.

He placed his hand on the back door and took a deep breath. He clutched his chest, attempting to steady his nerves. *Get it together, Mumtaz. Do what you came to do and get out.* Thunder shook the ground, traveling up his legs into his torso. The looming threat of rain and the darkening sky urged him to turn the knob on the door and go inside before he lost his nerve.

Mumtaz kicked himself for not leaving a light on inside the kitchen. His eyes darted back and forth, adjusting to the unfamiliar shapes of the cabinetry and cooking devices. He put on a pair of shooting gloves he found in the bag and ran his hand along the wall to find a light switch.

When the fluorescent overhead lights buzzed to life, he stepped further away from the door. He slipped one of the magazines into the Glock and dropped the remaining four into his pocket.

What the hell am I doing? It's one guy. Then again, better to be safe than sorry. He couldn't afford to waste more time. Chef Malcolm and the others may have suffered the same fate as Chef Anna and Chef Tomás. Thinking about the vicious little woman turned his blood cold.

He'd left her impaled and hanging on the broom handle, too afraid to touch her corpse, fearing she had played at dying. Mumtaz eased down the counter, dropping the gun bag on one of them along the way.

The mop sink sat at the next corner on the right. He steeled his nerves to see her dead body again. He needed to see it. It would help him prepare to face Chef Tomás. He adjusted his grip on the gun and walked with purpose.

He arrived at the mop station and his head dropped. Everything bad that had happened in his life had been mostly his fault, but some of it was beyond his doing. Like this moment. Chef Dupree's body was gone, but how? *The fucking curse never lets up,* he thought.

A slight whimper escaped his lips when he spotted a trail of blood leading from the mop station to the other side of the cabinets. Thankful that she hadn't found him first, he had no choice but to follow it and find her. Mumtaz glanced behind him, just in case, then advanced into the belly of the kitchen.

More than one dark scenario entered his mind. What if she let Chef Tomás out? What if they escaped the restaurant and ran loose through the city? What if they were waiting to ambush him?

Leaving sounded good. But if he left, who would clean up his mess? The police? The army? Who would take responsibility for the chaos and pandemonium? Who did he expect to protect his family?

Mumtaz's mind flipped between fear and acceptance several times. The walkway forked to the left, which led to the dining room, and to the right, where the freezer stood, eerily quiet. He assumed that Chef Tomás had calmed down without a victim to provoke him. *Maybe I got lucky, and he died.* Or maybe he had gotten out. Either way, a bloody trail veered to the left. He followed it.

Finding her wasn't difficult. He tilted his head when he heard the smacking noises coming from her office. *Shit.* Whatever demonic forces had affected the salt were still drawing her to it.

Mumtaz walked, light as a feather to the office door. The broken broom handle jutted out from her back as she sat knee-deep in the ripped bags of salt, oblivious to the world around her. Mumtaz had a clear shot but didn't want to use the gun. Rousing Chef Tomás before he came up with a plan wasn't a good idea.

He doubled back to the dishwashing area and did a thorough search for something he could use as a weapon. Disappointed, he headed around the cabinets to the other aisle. It too sat bare and sterile, save for streaked, bloody shoe prints from earlier. Mumtaz walked to the end of the aisle, exploring the cabinets as he went. He got to the last one, then backed up. *Jackpot.*

The butcher room sat untouched and uncleaned since things had taken an unintended turn for the worst. A cow's head rotted on the cutting table, and to Mumtaz's relief, a host of assorted knives and cutting instruments sat next to it. He picked up a ten-inch cleaver to get a feel for it, versus the seven-inch blade. It felt too heavy and difficult to wield in his hand.

He set it down on the table and took the smaller chopper, along with a ten-inch butcher knife with a curved blade. Mumtaz zipped his leather jacket to the base of his throat. She wasn't getting to him this time if he could help it.

He tucked the Glock and holster into his pants and headed back to Chef Anna's office with the butcher knife in his left hand and the cleaver in his right. Fear sent shivers down his spine.

His body went rigid. The thought of killing a person that he had been so sure was dead made him question his sanity. If he'd had to wager, he would have bet every dime he had that he would find her body where he'd left it.

A loud bang from the opposite end of the kitchen jolted him. Adrenaline surged in his veins as he fought to regain his composure. Thunder continued rolling across the city, shaking the foundation of the building as it passed overhead.

Mumtaz heard the howling wind, courtesy of the now open back door. Had she gotten outside? *Sonofabitch.*

He pivoted and ran towards the door, afraid for his life, but more worried about the repercussions if Chef Anna got loose in the city. Mumtaz tore through the back and side alleys, then to the front of the restaurant. No one was on the street.

He doubled back to the alley, circling the area until he was satisfied that she wasn't out there. The streetlights swung overhead, wild and menacing in the wind.

A green tint loomed in the dark sky, and he changed his mind about wanting a tornado to come and prayed that no funnel clouds formed. The world couldn't handle two calamities at once, even if one might destroy the other. It could also pick them up and deposit them in the middle of the city.

Mumtaz got back to the office, adjusting his grip on the knives. Chef Anna wasn't there. *Shit. Where could she be now?*

With his back against the narrow strip of wall between her office and the dining room, he glanced down both aisles of the kitchen to make sure they hadn't circled one another. Raindrops pelted the restaurant's roof, beating against the rhythm of his heart pounding in his chest.

The hairs on the back of his neck stood and he wiped sweat from his left brow with the sleeve of his jacket. Mumtaz lowered his arm. Intuition propelled him away from the porthole door, towards the freezers. Out of nowhere, Chef Anna lunged at him with her claws extended.

He recovered and plunged the butcher knife into her right side, leaving it deep within her body cavity, but she reacted as if she had no pain receptors whatsoever. Mumtaz couldn't figure out what compelled her to keep moving. His body and mind seemed to detach from one another, like he was watching the action from somewhere else.

Why was she still alive? A voice in his head screamed the answer. *It was the curse.* He dodged her attacks, jumping on top of the nearest stainless-steel cabinet to avoid the aggressive onslaught. She tried coming after him, but the broom handle caught on the lip of the cabinets behind her. Chef Anna swiped at him with her razor-sharp nails, froth dripping from her snapping mouth.

Mumtaz burst into a quick sprint as he watched what was once a viable and shrewd business woman try to tear out his throat. Her face was unrecognizable now; gray, burned, and caked with salt, along with blood-red eyes. Hellish.

He tossed the cleaver back and forth in his hands, trying to decide. Which was the best way to attack: bury it in her skull or go for the neck, lopping off the whole damned thing?

Chef Anna refused to slow down and give him time to think. She came for him, and his body took over where his mind failed. He slid in the sticky gore on the tiled flooring and pivoted. His arm swung around, burying the cleaver deep in the side of her head. He heard the crack of skull bones as the blade sunk into the soft tissues underneath, stopping her cold in her tracks.

Chef Anna's mouth snapped at him a final time, then she crumpled in a heap on the floor. Mumtaz stood above her on the counter and wondered. Could he trust that she was down for good?

He took the Glock out of the holster and pointed it at her. Mumtaz watched the texture of her skin morph before his eyes, returning to its former human properties. Sorrow ached within him for the life he helped destroy.

He hadn't cared for the woman on a deeper level, but he didn't want her to die. And now, he had to make certain that she had died. For good. She'd fooled him once already; he couldn't let it happen again. That didn't make pulling the trigger any easier.

His fingers hesitated to squeeze it. He needed a sign. The rise and fall of her chest. The flutter of an eyelid or tremble of a lip. Mumtaz waited and watched. His ears pricked at the distant sound of thunder, and he noticed for the first time that the storm had come and gone. No tornadoes. He thanked Allah for small miracles. Then, Chef Tomás burst out of the freezer.

Mumtaz pivoted and shot Chef Tomás six times in the chest,

bringing him to the floor. A final bullet to the brain shut him down. It happened so fast, he hadn't had time to think. He shot him again in the head to be sure, then jumped the counter and did the same to Chef Anna.

He stood there shaking with the gun in his hand. Jasim had taken him to the range enough that he knew how to use it, but there was a big difference in paper targets and flesh. Blood seeped out from their bodies and the gunshot wounds smoked.

Mumtaz placed the Glock in the holster, careful of the smoking barrel, and studied them. There was no way to tell if they were dead or not. *Fuck it.* He grabbed a mini torch from one of the cabinets, lighter fluid, and a stack of kitchen towels, which he stuffed near the gas canister on the fryer. He grabbed Jasim's bag off the counter and ran for his vehicle. He drove three blocks away and listened. When the glass blew out of the surrounding buildings from the blast, he drove away.

Chapter Nineteen

Mumtaz drove down the highway as firetrucks and police raced past him in the opposite direction. It was pouring. He hoped the rain didn't interfere with the fire at Dupree's. He wanted all the evidence pointing to him to go up in smoke.

His cellphone rang. Who was calling now? It couldn't be Mo. He'd shattered her phone on the sidewalk, and Jasim wouldn't call this soon. He read the call display and sighed.

"Hey Aminah."

"Hey cousin, how's it going?" The sweet disposition of her voice normally warmed his heart, but even Aminah couldn't settle his nerves tonight.

"Not good."

"Did I catch you at a bad time?"

"Sort of. I'm feeling out of sorts at the moment." Understatement of the year.

"I have some news that might cheer you up," Aminah said.

He doubted it. "What's up?"

"You know how you love being an uncle, right?"

"Yeah."

"Get ready to step up your game, Mumtaz. Reza and I are having twins."

"What?" Mumtaz grinned from ear to ear despite his current situation. "Aminah, that's crazy. Congratulations. It couldn't happen to a nicer person."

"Aww, thank you." She paused. "Are those sirens?"

"It's the television." He winced at the lie. "Anyway, maybe now you'll chill and delegate some work to your staff. You could use a break."

"I'm fine, Mumtaz."

"Are you? I remember how happy you used to be when you were catering, and you haven't smiled like that since you opened this place. I can't imagine how much harder running a new restaurant will be in your condition. Twins! I can't believe it." The good news hit him hard. Being an uncle had its rewards, but being a father was a different ball game. His eyes closed, and for a moment, he imagined Mo in Aminah's place, calling to tell him the good news. Imagine, blessed with not one, but two.

"Mumtaz, you know it's not in my nature to chill. In fact, I'm thinking about going to the restaurant right now."

He perked up. "Now? Why would you do that, Aminah? It's close to midnight."

"Your mom and sister left ages ago, and I can't sleep. Reza's out of town again. I have some recipes I'd like to work on, and…"

Panic rose inside of him. There was no way in hell he could let her go there tonight. "Aminah, please. I'm glad that you shared your amazing news, but I need you to slow down and think of your babies. You need to be strong for them. Stay home and get some rest. Besides, who goes out when there's a tornado watch?"

"It's been downgraded to occasional heavy rain. The sky is opening up. Mumtaz, I'm perfectly capable of…"

"Aminah, please!" He caught sight of his face in the rearview mirror. His hair and face shone slick in the reflection, coated with a sheen of sweat. "I would never forgive myself if something happened to you. Please, stay home."

"Is this your curse stuff again?"

"No. It's your big cousin being protective," he said. "Just go to bed, okay? Spare me from having to worry about you."

"Fine. I'll go first thing in the morning, weirdo."

He let out a deep sigh of relief. "Thank you."

"You're welcome," she said. "Love you, cousin. Thanks for putting up with me."

"Love you too, and we both know it's the other way around."

"Goodnight, Uncle Mumtaz."

"Goodnight."

He hung up the phone and immediately dialed Brimstones's Grille.

"Come on, pick up." It went straight to voicemail for the third time.

He darted in and out of traffic, shaving off half the time of the thirty-minute drive. The near-empty parking lot made him feel a lot better. The less witnesses, the better. With the Glock planted on his hip in the holster, and his jacket pockets full of extra magazines, he sneaked behind the restaurant into the cobblestone alley.

The unlit back of Andalusia stood ominous in the glow of Brimstone's lights. Thank God Aminah didn't come. Brimstone looked down on him like the eyes of a giant jack-o-lantern, the open door a mouth, awaiting its prey. Mumtaz used caution as he stepped across the threshold into the disheveled kitchen.

The mess inside Brimstone's Grille went beyond that of a typical afternoon and busy dinner rush. Smashed food, crumbs, and blood blanketed the entire floor. Each crunch under Mumtaz's shoes made his heart lurch in fear. There was no way to be quiet and nowhere to hide. He kept his gun at the ready, conscious of the steaming tables and whirring overhead fans. The humidity made him sweat and the skin on his arms and back broke out in prickly gooseflesh when the timed fan above the workstations kicked in.

He tried recalling the conversation from earlier. Chef Malcolm told him that Eduardo, the senior chef, had taken a nosedive under the counters. If the salt affected Eduardo the same way it had with Chefs Anna and Tomás, Mumtaz needed to find him first. He flicked the switch, cutting off the fans, then pricked up his ears.

The blades of the fans came to a squeaking halt. Besides the humming electric currents near the freezers, Mumtaz didn't hear a sound. He hoped he wouldn't have to play hide-and-seek all night with these guys. It was better when they made themselves known and came out to fight.

As his feet crunched down the aisles of the kitchen, he ducked every few feet and scanned the underside of the cabinets. The trail of blood-encrusted food thinned, and there were visible sections of seamless flooring near the prep tables, covered in a thin layer of pink-tinged salt.

The trail of pink salt, mixed with the blood of an unfortunate victim, grew darker and richer in color before it took a detour across the kitchen. It got lost in a large puddle of reddish-black muck before disappearing underneath the counter in the far corner. Was Eduardo under there? Had he procured a trap for his unwitting victims?

The lighting made it difficult to see what lay beneath, but Mumtaz did his best by crouching and studying the area near it. The dried skin on his back popped open along the seam of his fresh scabs, itching, and burning. He breathed, inhaling, and exhaling in quick, heavy bursts until the pain subsided. The quiet in the kitchen maddened him.

Where the hell are they? As if on cue, Mumtaz's ringtone broke the silence. He tried to silence the ringer on the cellphone but fumbled, dropping it to the floor. With a deft hand, he swiped it up off the floor and answered it.

"Hello?" he asked in a curt whisper.

"Where the hell are you, Mumtaz? I want my money."

"Luqman, I'm nearby. I'll be with you in a minute, okay? I have some urgent business to tend to."

"What are you talking about, Mumtaz? I'm the urgent bus—"

Mumtaz cut the phone call short and turned off the ringer, but it was too late. The dining room door burst open. Rosie came in, growling and scanning the kitchen. He cowered in the corner behind an open cabinet door, uttering a silent prayer. *Please, God, please.*

Her teeth opened and closed with a chomping sound. She moved deeper into the kitchen and the door flew open behind her. A low moan escaped Mumtaz's lips and he clamped a hand over his mouth. Rosie turned in his direction and hissed.

The sight of Chef Malcolm stumbling through the doors, strangely animated, as if he were a puppet on a string, disturbed him. Someone rearranged the man's face and forgot to put his ears where they belonged, leaving them dangling near his shoulders, held on by the lobes. Seeing the mangled chef in his current state threw his mind into disorder. They had spoken just a couple of hours ago. And now, he was a gruesome wretch, looking to destroy whoever got in his way.

Mumtaz needed to hide. He didn't want to take them both on at the same time; their combined strength and speed might overpower him. He didn't have room to make mistakes. For now, he planned to squeeze inside the cabinet and wait for his moment.

Mumtaz kept his eyes on them while he removed items from the cabinet with his left hand, making the least amount of noise that he could. A hand shot out and grabbed him around the wrist. His bladder released, wetting the thighs of his pants. The hand covered his mouth before he could scream. Eduardo.

He looked like death, but he looked human enough that Mumtaz kept his wits. His finger pressed against his lips, and Mumtaz nodded. Eduardo let him go and pushed open the other cabinet door. There was enough room for Mumtaz to crawl inside if he could do it without disturbing the stacks of sheet pans.

The two men worked together, with Eduardo holding the pans still as Mumtaz scrunched and crawled into the steel box. It hurt, and the pans dug into his shins, but he'd take sore legs over a double-teamed mauling any day. He closed the cabinet door a tiny bit, then nodded at Eduardo.

They sat still, listening to Chefs Rosie and Malcolm, clicking, and chomping their teeth. They seemed to be clicking in patterns. *Are they communicating?*

When his eyes adjusted to the dark, Mumtaz saw Eduardo flexing and relaxing his feet to wake them up. How long had he been inside the cabinet and why didn't he make a run for it? And where was Chef Tampa? Was the blood puddle near the cabinets remnants of him?

Both men jumped as something rolled along the floor next to the cabinets. Mumtaz held his breath as Chef Rosie and Chef Malcolm growled and moved closer. His heart rate shot through the roof.

He heard one of them approach the open cabinet door and he held his breath. Mumtaz aimed the gun at an awkward angle, hoping to shoot down whoever it was if they made a move. It made no difference which one he sent to Hell as long as he didn't screw it up.

Mumtaz detected motion from the corner of his eye and turned his head. He and Eduardo watched as a red potato rolled across the floor from somewhere in the back of the kitchen. The chefs growled.

Mumtaz and Eduardo glanced at one another in confusion. A second and third potato tumbled across the floor in the same direction. The chefs followed after them.

Mumtaz opened his cabinet door, careful not to call attention to himself, then peeked out. Chef Tampa waved from behind a barrel of potatoes. Mumtaz brandished his handgun and noted the chef's expression of relief on his pallid, sweaty face. Blood ran from an open wound in his torso, and he didn't look well, but at least he was still on their side.

He lifted his head above the cabinet door and saw Chefs Rosie and Malcolm staring at the potatoes. A sigh of relief escaped Mumtaz's lips. As long as they kept their backs turned, he could climb out of the cabinet and give his legs some relief.

He opened the door wider and exited, then helped Eduardo climb out. The poor man's side had been ribboned by a set of sharp claws and what was left of his apron was stained brown and crimson. Mumtaz wondered how he wasn't screaming from the pain, but he didn't ask.

They slid around to the back of the kitchen and Tampa joined them. He had a gleaming stainless-steel cleaver in his hands. From the looks of it, he hadn't summoned the courage to use it yet.

Eduardo reached into his pocket and plucked out a baggie with white powder. Mumtaz tensed. Eduardo sensed his trepidation and patted Mumtaz's shoulder. *Not salt*, he mouthed, before he snorted some of the white substance up his nostril.

Now, he understood why he wasn't screaming. *He's high as a kite.* Eduardo offered him some, but Mumtaz refused. He liked weed, but hard drugs scared him. Besides, now was the time he needed his wits the most.

Mumtaz's pocket buzzed and Eduardo and Tampa's expressions changed to dread. Tampa tossed another potato in Rosie and Malcolm's direction. Mumtaz reached inside and powered off the phone for good. No more interruptions; humans could wait.

Mumtaz met Tampa's eyes and nodded towards Rosie and Malcolm. Tampa shook his head and hugged the cleaver to his chest. He wasn't ready. Eduardo snatched it away from him and nodded at Mumtaz. He hoped the coke running through Eduardo's veins gave him the boost he needed. It was time to take care of business.

Chapter Twenty

MUMTAZ LED the sneak attack on the chefs. It was only fair, considering he had the gun. He thanked Allah that he wasn't alone this time. Who would believe him without seeing it?

They started up the service line, easing along the gritty floor. Mumtaz turned and pointed to Chef Tampa, who opted to stay behind, then jabbed his finger at the overhead fans. *Turn them on*, he mouthed. The useless idiot refused.

Incensed, Mumtaz gestured for Eduardo to stay put until he could circle back and come down the opposite aisle. If they both turned on the overhead fans, they could move closer without being found out.

When he reached the opposite side of the counter, he pointed to Eduardo, then lifted his index finger and began counting to three. Eduardo glanced towards the other end of the kitchen, nervous, then returned his attention to Mumtaz.

Mumtaz lifted his second finger and took a deep breath. When the fans came on, he planned to rush forward and plant bullets deep in their skulls. If things went according to plan, he wouldn't need Eduardo's help at all. If not, he knew what to do with that cleaver.

Mumtaz lifted his third finger and in the split second before he or Eduardo could flip the switches, a terrible crash of pots and lids hit the floor. They turned towards the source of the noise and Mumtaz's jaw dropped.

"You sonofabitch!" Mumtaz said.

"Sorry guys, I'm sorry." Chef Tampa ran towards the service door, intent on fleeing the restaurant without them.

Chef Rosie pounced, and Mumtaz stumbled across the smooth floor with her on his back. He cried out as a patch of hair tore away from his scalp, leaving his head exposed and bloody. His hands covered the injury, and she continued her abuse, shredding his shooting gloves, shirt, wrists, and fingers. Her attack forced him to squeeze the trigger and a bullet ricocheted off one stainless surface to another.

Mumtaz heard a thwack, and she fell away from him, hitting the floor hard. He grimaced as he scrambled away from her and to his feet. He looked down at the chef. Her eyes gazed into whatever place the angels had carried her soul as blood trickled from the smoking hole in her temple.

"MashaAllah," he said, marveling at his good fortune. Maybe Aminah was right. Curses were nonsense.

"Taz, help!" Eduardo jumped from one counter to another with Chef Malcolm hot on his trail. Mumtaz brought the Glock up with both hands, aiming at the chef's torso. He locked into position and squeezed the trigger in quick succession, knocking Chef Malcolm to the floor.

Eduardo jumped off the counter and grabbed him by the arm. "Let's get the fuck out of here, man." Mumtaz hesitated. He didn't want the chef to get loose in the streets, but shooting in this part of the kitchen could prove fatal to all of them.

He jumped across the overturned rack, following behind Eduardo, who headed towards the alley. Mumtaz caught up to him and slid to the ground, avoiding a near-collision with Eduardo's backside. Chef Tampa hadn't gone far.

Cloaked in shadow, Mumtaz saw Tampa's body contorting in the alley. He was one of them now. Eduardo turned on his heels, picking Mumtaz up from the ground.

They took a hard left, avoiding Chef Malcolm, who had a gaping hole in his chest. Mumtaz used the butt of the Glock to smash Aminah's office windows. The sound of the alarm deafened them. They climbed inside and stumbled through the door, making their way into the kitchen of Andalusia. If Mumtaz never saw another commercial kitchen in his life, it would be too soon.

$$\sim$$

CHEFS MALCOLM and Tampa shattered the remaining glass climbing into the window after them. Mumtaz and Eduardo barricaded the office door with a small kitchen island, then ran for cover in the dining room. The chefs broke through the flimsy barrier within seconds and were in pursuit of them once more.

"This way," Eduardo said, ducking under a table. Mumtaz crawled in beside him just as Tampa entered the room. The blaring alarm competed with Mumtaz's pounding headache. "The cops are going to come and save us," Eduardo assured him.

Mumtaz wasn't so sure. Chef Malcolm darted into the dining room from the kitchen. He charged the windows at the front entrance, banging his head into the glass, the same way Chef Tomás had done to the freezer door. It didn't take much for it to give.

"He's trying to get out," Mumtaz said. "I have to stop him before he does. Eduardo, you go after Chef Tampa, while I take him out. Eduardo?"

Mumtaz glanced at Eduardo and his spirits fell. He'd fallen backwards against the legs of a dining chair. His eyes rolled until the whites showed and his mouth grew frothy. Claws pushed out of his fingertips, and his hands stretched like burgeoning branches of a young tree in spring.

Eduardo twisted and morphed into something beyond human. His body turned black, and pustules exploded on the surface of his skin. Mumtaz sat there, transfixed by the chef's horrid transformation. Chef Tampa knocked over the hostess podium and brought Mumtaz back to reality. He needed to get the hell out of here.

The cops were bound to show up soon in a neighborhood like this, and he didn't want to be here to explain the dead or undead bodies. He felt conflicted, but the time for trust and taking chances had passed. Mumtaz rolled out from under the table, lifted the Glock and shot Eduardo in the head.

Chefs Tampa and Malcolm followed the noise and gave chase. Mumtaz headed into the kitchen for a final showdown. He dropped the magazine from the Glock and reloaded it with a fresh one from his jacket pocket.

Chef Tampa tackled him and bit deep into his left hamstring, locking his joints. He dropped the handgun and tightened his fists. Pain blurred his vision, and he clenched his teeth as tears streamed from his eyes.

Chef Malcolm sprawled across him, fighting Chef Tampa for access to his body. He bit down hard on Mumtaz's shoulder, and he howled from the excruciating pain. Chef Malcolm came away with a chunk of his flesh and the bite burned like he'd been injected with fire. Crystals of salt mixed with his blood and burned in his veins, traveling up his arm, into his neck.

His heart fluttered in his chest and the light seemed to fade. Breathing became difficult. Every moment, his body struggled to function. He wanted to give up and give in. Mumtaz collapsed and they bit into him, cutting, and gnashing with their teeth.

The poison spread through him, burning him from the inside out. His skin went flush and broke out in beads of sweat. Death was in the air. Mumtaz felt certain. But he couldn't let them survive. Not here in his cousin's restaurant. Not anywhere in the city. He pried his eyes open and searched for the gun.

It lay just out of reach, under the stove. He stretched his fingers towards the gun until they shook. Tampa bit a chunk from his forearm and his hand retracted. Mumtaz flipped onto his back and kicked Chef Malcolm into the water table, then scooted away from Chef Tampa.

He grabbed the gun and fought to hold it steady in his trembling, weakened hands. Chef Tampa bared his teeth and dove at him. Mumtaz aimed and squeezed the trigger. Tampa fell on him and went still. Bits of brain matter and skull fragments coated the stainless-steel panels near the stove.

Chef Malcolm clambered out from the empty water table and swiped his claws in Mumtaz's direction. He missed, and Mumtaz fired at him, hitting him in the torso and shoulders. It was enough to get away.

The chef chased after him, and Mumtaz hobbled through the kitchen, back towards the service door. Chef Malcolm sliced through a series of wires near the door and sparks flew, igniting stacks of cardboard boxes. Mumtaz turned the door handle and escaped into the night air. The chef lunged at him, taking him down to the pavement. Shots rang out in the alleyway and Chef Malcolm went limp.

Mumtaz sat up and wiped blood and tears from his eyes. "Thank God you're here. I couldn't have kept him away much longer—" The rest of his acknowledgements stuck in his throat as the air around him exploded several times. Blood bubbled in his throat, and he could taste it. Stunned, Mumtaz sank back to the pavement, unable to move. A dark figure stood over him, casting a shadow from the streetlights. His body felt cold.

"You're late, bitch." The glow of a blazing fire shone in the man's wild eyes. Mumtaz recognized the voice. He tried to speak but couldn't.

"SubhanAllah, what the hell happened here tonight?" asked the man. He pulled down the hood of his jacket as the rain let up. Mumtaz coughed and the taste of copper filled his mouth. He watched as the man fished the vial of salt from his pocket. "What do we have here?"

"Is he still alive, Hamza?"

"I guess so, but he looks nearly dead."

"For the love of God, if you're going to be useless, get out of the way. I'll check for myself."

Mumtaz watched Hamza step aside for Luqman. His body shivered violently, despite the angry flames licking the doorway above his head, but he didn't mind; at least the pain was gone.

"Mumtaz, what did you get yourself into? Everybody's going to think I had something to do with this," Luqman said. He clicked his tongue and lifted Mumtaz's jacket away from him. "I hope you didn't get into trouble on my account, Taz. I never would have hurt you or Jasim this badly. A couple of fingers is nothing."

At long last, the sound of sirens wailing in the distance filled Mumtaz's ears. It didn't matter if the police came now. The curse was finished. He wished Mo had kept the baby. He always wanted a son. He mustered enough energy to lift his hands and look at the smooth palms. Both lifelines were gone. They dropped to his sides, and he sighed.

"I hope you've said your peace, Mumtaz. It's time for Allah to take you home," Luqman said, placing a hand on his forehead. Mumtaz couldn't feel it. Had he not been dying, he would have told Jasim about Luqman's attentive, gentle nature. Jasim would have called him a liar. Then again, Luqman would never have revealed that side of himself had he thought Mumtaz had a chance in hell of surviving.

He closed his eyes and thought about sleep. He felt at peace and looked forward to resting. Life drained out of his limbs and the darkness took him under. He thought he felt Luqman's hands in his jacket pockets, but he couldn't be certain. If so, he most likely found the magazines, car keys and the envelope with his name written on it.

"Shit." Luqman checked the money for bullet holes and shook his head. "What do you know? The unlucky bastard had all of my money," he said, thumbing through the bills. "No bullet holes. How lucky."

"Hey, what's this?" Hamza asked. "It tastes good. I mean, really good," Hamza said, licking his finger and tasting the salt.

"Give it to me," Luqman said. He shook the vial and had a little taste of the white substance inside. "I've never had this kind of blow before, but it's damn good stuff." He tapped out a little on his hand and snorted it. "This is phenomenal. Try some, Hamza." He passed the vial back to his cousin. "I guess tonight's my lucky night. Now, let's get his body out of here and bury it before the cops get here."

"What about this other guy?"

"Grab him too. He's got your bullets in him."

"In the salt caves?" Hamza asked, snorting the salt granules.

"Where else?"

Neither of them noticed the tall Black man in the white coat slipping out from the shadows behind them. Two quick taps to the head with the gun in his hand and Luqman and Hamza fell over onto the pavement next to Chef Malcolm.

"I warned you," Lebe said. "There are consequences if things get out of control." Lebe gave Mumtaz a long, hard stare. The gun went off and Mumtaz's head bounced. Life seeped out of him, but before it did, he thought he saw Lebe morph into a hideous black and white bird and fly away. *A pied crow.* That couldn't be right. Either way, it wasn't his problem anymore.

Epilogue

MONET HADN'T REPLACED her cellphone, but a sinking feeling that bad news was on its way lingered. She sat at a table in the hospital cafeteria on break when a black dog pacing under a streetlamp in the parking lot confirmed her suspicions. An omen. Someone she loved was dead.

A massive winged shadow cast itself across the dog as a black and white bird landed in the grass near the bushes. Monet sighed in relief. It was bad news, but at least her father was okay. No one else in the cafeteria saw Lebe's shape shift from a pied crow into the form of a tall, slim man, black as coal, wearing a long, white jacket and black suit.

He watched his daughter through the glass and his jaw clamped down the way it did when he grew tired of her shenanigans. Monet rolled her eyes at him, not in the mood for a lecture. His fingers called her to him, and she swiped her ID tag off the table and met him outside.

"Hey," she said, folding her arms over her scrubs.

"Hey yourself. See that?" he asked, pointing to the black dog skulking near the ambulance entrance.

"Yeah, I see it," she said.

"Your boyfriend's dead."

"There was nothing I could do for him. That curse was an ancient one beyond my scope. Mumtaz had it coming anyway. He couldn't stay out of trouble."

"You don't sound choked up about it," Lebe said. She shrugged. "That's cold, Monet. You let the man die believing you killed his child."

"I was angry at the time. If I had suspected he'd die so soon, I wouldn't have lied about it," she said, clutching her middle. Something in Lebe's handsome, wrinkled face gave her pause. Monet had no idea how old her father was, but his sense of mischief seemed to increase with age. "You're the one who told him to sell the salt in the first place, aren't you? How can you chastise me when you've had a hand in his death too?"

"What can I say? I'm an agent of chaos. Besides, I thought you'd catch him red-handed and break up. I had no idea the idiot would actually sell it."

"That was mean, Lebe."

"Perhaps, but I tried to spare him the heartache of dealing with you. He wasn't the only one you lied to. You also told me that you were getting an abortion." He pointed to her belly. "Still pregnant, no?"

"Look, Lebe, you're my dad, but I'm a grown woman. If I change my mind about getting an abortion, that's my choice."

"Chère. You're a Tansy. Pregnancy steals your magic. All your spells will be rotten."

"Maybe I'm different."

"You're not. It happened to your mother, and it's happening to you. As long as you carry that baby inside you, your magic will fail."

"It won't."

Lebe cracked a smile. "You sound just like her."

"I'm not like my mother. You'll see. My magic won't fail."

"Oh? Then explain why your true love is dead."

"It's like I said. Mumtaz had it coming to him."

Lebe's head tilted. "I'm not talking about Mumtaz."

Monet raced inside the hospital and hopped into the elevator. She pressed the basement floor button, then smashed the close door button. "Come on, damn you." The doors squeaked shut and the car lurched, then made its way downstairs.

She paced the length of the car as the ancient contraption lowered itself into the belly of the hospital. Lebe told her things that she found impossible to believe. Dread flooded her system, but unless she confirmed it with her own eyes, none of what Lebe alluded to was true. The elevator hit the bottom floor and the doors peeled open.

When there was enough room to squeeze through, Monet darted from the car and sprinted down the hall. She used her ID tag to sign into the morgue, then checked the sign-in roster.

Two bodies had come in while she was on her break. *Black, Andrew Allen*, and *Hanzlik, Norman Daryl*. Hot tears made parallel streams down her cheeks, but she refused to believe what the roster told her. It had to be a mistake.

She walked to the coolers and slid open the drawer with Detective Norman Hanzlik's body inside. "Shit, baby. What happened to you?" She ran her fingers through the dead man's hair. "I told you to be careful."

A series of bruised needle punctures on the side of his neck caught her eye and she turned his head. The muscles had begun to stiffen and that made her cry harder. In an hour or so, he'd be hard as a rock. Being a nurse, she expected it, but seeing it happen to someone she loved was too much to bear.

Norman should have been protected by her magic. He should be alive. Lebe was right. The bastard child in her belly had caused her magic to fail. But she couldn't get rid of it. She loved it already, as her mother had loved her.

"I'm sorry, love. This is all my fault." Monet leaned over and kissed him on the lips. "They won't get away with this. You'll have your revenge, I swear."

～

A FEW DAYS LATER, after explosive bouts of grief and morning sickness, Monet emerged from her self-imposed isolation and went back to work. She kept a close eye on the girl in the room with the uniformed cop stationed outside the door. When the sexy Black cop with the freckles left, Monet lured the uniformed idiot away with a little help from her favorite jinni. He followed the woman in red into the stairway, quiet and entranced.

Don't kill him, Monet had instructed. She only needed a few moments for what she came to do. The girl was asleep, dreaming and drenching the bed with anxiety. Monet could smell fear in her sweat.

She leaned over her and whispered in her ear. "It's going to get much, much worse. When the time is right, I'm coming for you." Monet straightened up, placed a black tulip in Haleema's hand, then walked out of the room. She was feeling salty, but revenge was going to be so sweet.

The End.

AFTERWORD

Thank you for reading Salarius, I hope you found it as enjoyable to read as it was to write. Mumtaz and Monet were the real stars of the show, but I have to say, Lebe begs me to be a frontrunner in his own adventures from time to time. Who knows?

Don't forget to leave a review, we indie authors need the support more than you know!

ACKNOWLEDGMENTS

I'd like to thank my older children for lending me their ears on multiple occasions. I've learned that while they are brutally honest, they are also patient as I bounce from one idea to the next.

A big thanks to Edet Nsikak for boosting my confidence. You're an awesome beta reader.

To the readers who told me to hurry up: I hope you enjoyed what I delivered.

Nakia Cook is a Black American expat living in Canada with her husband and five children.

Through her writing, she hopes to introduce diverse characters from the Muslim and African Diasporas to horror and fantasy readers.

Sign up for Nakia's newsletter for title and cover reveals and information about new releases once in a while.

nakiacook.com

www.ingramcontent.com/pod-product-compliance
Lightning Source LLC
Chambersburg PA
CBHW030932060726
47591CB00005B/1763